THE LAST ASSIGNMENT

A Novel by

John W. Gemmer

CCB Publishing
British Columbia, Canada

The Last Assignment: A Novel

Copyright ©2013 by John W. Gemmer
ISBN-13   978-1-77143-043-2
First Edition

Library and Archives Canada Cataloguing in Publication
Gemmer, John W., 1948-
The last assignment : a novel / written by John W. Gemmer.
ISBN 978-1-77143-043-2
Also available in electronic format.
Additional cataloguing data available from Library and Archives Canada

Cover artwork: Man with dreadlocks: © Micropix | CanStockPhoto.com
Home burglary: © Mike2focus | Dreamstime.com
Fixing an attacker: © Josef Philipp | iStockphoto.com

Publisher: CCB Publishing
             British Columbia, Canada
             www.ccbpublishing.com

Dedication

I'm dedicating this book to the memory of June Elaine Gemmer, my mother, who encouraged me to write in the fourth grade. She was an avid reader and studied English at Sullins College, Bristol, Virginia, sometime in the early 1930s. My first book was similar to the type of stories found in the popular *Hardy Boys* series I read as a child.

Acknowledgements

I wrote a rough draft of this story in 1998-1999 and finished a first edit in 2000, after which I put the work on hold until 2012 when I decided to finish the project.

Along the way, I was encouraged to write this manuscript as a retirement project by family and friends.

Special thanks to Kevin Sheets and Gerry Hertzler, who helped edit the book and Roger Sellers and Gary Cochrane, who provided some of the Vietnam background information.

Chapter 1

He pushed himself away from the table and, staggering a little, made his way to the door, slyly pocketing the tips from a couple of tables along the way. He was tired and drunk, and he wanted to replenish his stash.

His old Vespa was propped against a railing in front of the bar and he straddled it awkwardly, coughing along with the sputtering, noisy engine as it started.

The rush of sea air sobered him slightly as he followed the north shore road out of town. In the pale moonlight, he could see the outlines of the vacation houses on the hills above the ocean. Fancy homes for wealthy people who used them only a few weeks during the year. Strawberry resented the apparent ease of their lives.

A small house on the hillside, partially hidden by palms and overgrown vegetation, attracted his attention. He had noticed it on the ride into Christiansted earlier in the day. It was one of the newer houses on this part of the island and Strawberry had watched it gradually take shape on the site months earlier. He didn't know if it was occupied.

Deciding to take a closer look, Strawberry switched off the feeble headlamp of the cycle and turned off the shore road, following a narrow, winding driveway up the hill. The gravel crunched beneath the wheels. He cut the engine halfway up the drive and laid the Vespa on its side. He removed a rusty screwdriver from his tool kit and carefully approached the house.

The carport next to the house was empty; the home seemed still and unoccupied. Strawberry peered through the darkness trying to sense if anyone was inside. He was a little unsteady, but he trusted his instincts. Probably a vacation home for some rich Continental. There would be something inside he could sell; electronics for sure. He was unaware of the Jeep parked behind the house. Strawberry found an unscreened window and, working quickly with the screwdriver, pried it open and climbed inside. He hadn't done a home on this part of the island in a while.

Standing in a small pantry off the kitchen, he read the time on the microwave, 3:32. Congratulating himself on his stealth, he paused and carefully looked around before proceeding further in the house. A small stack of mail on the counter, caught his attention. His eyes were adjusting to the darkness; there was enough light for him to see through the kitchen into the living room. The bedrooms were probably on the other side of the house. He would check them first.

Slowly, he moved through the kitchen and into the living room, still carrying the screwdriver. Nothing in either room seemed out of place or menacing. In the living room, a half-opened door to the right caught his attention. He cautiously approached the door and slowly pushed it open and entered the room. Strawberry felt a cool breeze from an open window. The sight of an unmade bed surprised him.

*　　*　　*

The buzz of a moped from the shore road below awakened Jim Bartlett moments earlier. The buzzing sound, amplified by the humid early morning air, had approached and stopped. *Three thirty. Damn locals didn't believe in mufflers. Probably one of them leaving a Christiansted bar. Perhaps he'd gone off the road and into the sea. Good riddance.*

Bartlett closed his eyes but quickly opened them when he heard a muffled thud from the direction of the kitchen. Instantly, he was awake and alert.

Bartlett quietly got out of bed and moved to the side of the half-opened bedroom door. It didn't seem possible that Aguilar's people could have found him here; the path from New Orleans would have been difficult to follow. Still, a professional might take the chance this intruder was taking.

Bartlett had seen the shape of someone moving toward his bedroom. The person was carrying something resembling a knife in his left hand, he thought. Bartlett regretted that he hadn't grabbed the handgun from the nightstand. He would alert the intruder if he moved for it now. He flattened himself against the wall, next to the door, and waited.

He could smell the intruder and hear his breathing. *Rum, sweat and smoke.*

Slowly the door opened and Strawberry entered the bedroom. Bartlett attacked him immediately. He grabbed the man's left hand and violently twisted his wrist and arm up behind his back, spinning him around quickly. Strawberry grimaced with pain as his arm almost popped out of joint. The object clattered to the floor. With his free arm, Bartlett clutched the intruder from behind around the neck and began choking him. Strawberry fought to survive but he was not agile or strong enough to defend himself against Bartlett's maneuvers.

Moments later Strawberry weakened and Bartlett methodically snapped his neck. There was a dull cracking sound; Strawberry moaned and went limp. Bartlett let the body fall to the floor. A foot twitched erratically for a moment and then stopped. The scent of rum, sweat and smoke was in the air. The suddenness of death still surprised Bartlett.

Instinctively, he grabbed the 9 mm from the nightstand and carefully began a search of the house. Outside, he found the old Vespa in the driveway. It looked like a child's abandoned toy. He kicked it and cursed Strawberry. *Probably no one else. Not one of Aguilar's people. Just a stupid goddamn local, nerved up on rum and smoke, looking for valuables to pawn in Frederiksted, on the other side of the island.*

Returning to the house, he went to the bedroom and turned on the light. The dead man's eyes were wide open and glazed, his face contorted in an open-mouthed grimace; a young, good-looking black man with dreadlocks, wearing jeans, sneakers and a Miami Heat T-shirt. A weathered screwdriver lay on the floor beside the body. *The intruder is probably not more than 30 years old, if that. Stupid sonuvabitch.*

Bartlett loaded the body and the Vespa into the back of the Jeep. He used a weathered tarp and ties to secure the cargo. He started the Jeep and almost gagged. There was a sickening odor; Strawberry had shit his pants.

Chapter 2

A truck rumbling toward Christiansted on the shore road awoke Bartlett the next morning. His sleep was uneasy. The break-in reminded him of his vulnerability.

There were people who wanted to find him; at least one wanted to kill him. But it seemed unlikely that Aguilar or anyone else had tracked him to St. Croix. His path from Chicago to New Orleans to St. Croix would be very difficult to follow. However, Bartlett knew how determined a paid killer could be.

He looked at the 9 mm sitting on top of the nightstand. It reminded him of military duty in the Mekong Delta 32 years earlier. He was still leading a combat-ready existence and he realized he was weary of it. He slept lightly, as he had as an Army infantryman. 'Nam had transformed him. There he learned that he enjoyed the mortal danger of combat, and that he was quick and fearless in battle. After a brutal skirmish with the Vietcong in a nameless, muddy village, David Coles, the commanding officer, had told him, "You're either a natural-born killer or a natural-born soldier." Bartlett was flattered.

He could justify killing the intruder last night; Strawberry was an incidental victim caught in the wrong place at the wrong time. He made a fatal mistake and paid the ultimate price.

Also, Bartlett could justify the killings he performed contractually. He was a professional hired by criminals to get rid of other criminals, businessmen or politicians, who either screwed up or failed to cooperate with the mob. The victims generally had it coming and they knew the risks involved in getting out of line. *In this war, innocents were most always left alone.*

Bartlett sighed. He was struggling. He was ready for his wars to end.

For the first time in his life, he was comfortable. He wanted to remain in St. Croix and remain comfortable. His double life was tiring him and he knew too well that he wouldn't be impossible to find.

Sunlight poured into the room. The morning was already warm and humid when Bartlett got out of bed. A centipede crawling along the bedroom wall gracefully waved its legs, reminding Bartlett of a miniature conga line. There was no hint in the room of the struggle that occurred the night before.

Bartlett surveyed the room and acknowledged, almost ritually, the framed photograph of a dark-haired, dark-eyed woman with a pretty, narrow face. *Good morning Moira.*

The photograph was his only connection with her now; he wondered if and when they could be together again.

She had filled an empty space in his life. He felt now he could measure precisely the size of it. He replayed, as he had many times, the scene of his last night with her, before he left Chicago. The memory of her velvet skin, the fragrant scent of her hair and the firm shapeliness of her figure were vivid for Bartlett. The impossibility of being with her now made him ache.

He couldn't tell her why he'd left Chicago; couldn't tell her that he was leaving to protect her as well as himself. He'd left her a short note and money -- what one might leave a favorite whore. He couldn't imagine her response.

Again, he realized how important it was to bring her back into his life.

Chapter 3

Bartlett violated his own rule against local work when he accepted a totally unsuitable assignment in Chicago. However, it was a job he wanted to do. He had nursed a hatred of the pompous, power-hungry Alderman Leo Brezinski for many years.

Brezinski had betrayed striking mill workers years earlier resulting in the nearly fatal beating of Bartlett's father as he left a picket line. The workers had been loyal supporters of Brezinski, who promised police protection for the union. Bartlett remembered seeing his father in the tiny private hospital room looking old, weak and broken. Bartlett had vowed then he would never be so powerless as his father and he would always be able to protect himself.

Alderman Brezinski had foolishly reneged on a city contract promised to Bellini Brothers Construction. The Bellini brothers were unaccustomed to canceled contracts and to the manner in which Alderman Brezinski spoke to them. He told the Bellinis he was keeping their payoff money and he would arrange for other work later, and that they should forget this contract. The Bellini brothers' keen sense of business etiquette was violated. When they contacted Bartlett for a "consultation," he accepted their assignment readily. He would have done the job for free.

He stalked Brezinski for a week as he planned the hit. Bartlett wanted to face the alderman when he killed him. He knew his desire to show himself to the alderman was totally unnecessary and that it might compromise his safety and identity. However, he felt somehow compelled to have Brezinski see him, before he fired the final shot. He convinced himself by taking the Brezinski contract he would be avenging his father's beating.

The alderman lunched most days at a small Italian cafe on Roosevelt Road. His driver parked the bulky blue Cadillac directly in front of the restaurant and leaned on the fender and smoked until Brezinski was ready to leave. As a professional courtesy, Bartlett decided to kill the alderman after lunch rather than before thinking about the cliché, "The condemned man ate a hearty meal."

Brezinski's lunches usually lasted about 45 minutes and the alderman was true to form that day. As he emerged from the cafe in his shiny silk suit, Bartlett shouted, "Alderman, over here!" When the alderman turned to face him, Bartlett shot him twice, once in the head and once in the heart. Brezinski dropped like an unstrung puppet.

Suddenly, a big red-headed man ran out of the restaurant. He was carrying a gun. He leaped over

Brezinski's body and crouched in front of the blue Cadillac, where the driver was already hiding.

"Police!" he shouted. "Drop it!"

Bartlett trained his gun on the front of the Cadillac. He had no desire for a gunfight with a cop, but he would protect himself. As he backed slowly toward his car, he fired a warning shot into the rear window of the Cadillac, shattering it and the windshield. Then he jumped into his car and began to pull away in the opposite direction.

The red-haired man rose slowly in front of the Cadillac, his gun trained military-style on Bartlett's vehicle. He fired several rounds at the speeding vehicle before he put his service revolver down.

Their eyes had briefly been locked on each other for several seconds during the encounter. There was shock and recognition on both faces: Bartlett thought he had recognized Coles, his CO in Vietnam, and Coles thought he had recognized John Bartkowski, the quiet, intense young soldier who had been so coolly professional in battle.

Strangely, neither fired their guns with an intent to kill.

Bartlett was not completely certain it was Coles or that Coles recognized him, but he knew he would have to assume, at least, a cop had seen his face. He realized leaving the Windy City, temporarily, would be the best thing for him to do.

If it were Coles, Bartlett knew he would have some time. Coles' search would begin with John Bartkowski, who no longer existed. Bartkowski had carefully erased his past. When he returned from Vietnam for his mom's funeral, he realized that his life and the world had changed. And when he buried her next to his father and younger brother in the gloomy, crowded cemetery on Farwell Road, he decided to bury himself, too. Shortly after her funeral, he hired an attorney and legally changed his name to John Moore. And shortly before changing careers, he illegally became Jim Bartlett after ending John Moore's brief existence.

Now as he sped into the anonymous confusion of the downtown Chicago traffic, he knew he was leaving another life behind.

Leaving Moira would be his only regret.

Chapter 4

Moira Gray had appeared unexpectedly in Bartlett's life a year earlier on a Sunday afternoon at the Museum of Science and Industry, where he liked to leisurely walk and enjoy the exhibits. Bartlett enjoyed watching the visiting children marvel at some of the exhibits. He admired their curiosity, spontaneity and innocence and he felt a connection to his own childhood.

In the coffee shop, Bartlett turned too quickly trying to avoid rowdy children and accidentally bumped into a short, attractive woman, spilling her coffee. When he apologized and offered a replacement, she invited him to join her.

Bartlett was captivated by her in a way he thought he couldn't be. She was intense, intelligent and sensual. She sparked emotions he had either ignored or forgotten. Gray, 45, divorced and childless, seemed to be experiencing similar feelings. She thought Bartlett seemed polite, attractive and sexy.

Bartlett lived in an obscure apartment complex just inside the Loop and Moira owned a neat little house in Evanston. After several months of dating, they were spending most nights together in Evanston. On Mondays and Fridays, he would return to his downtown apartment to collect his mail and retrieve clean clothes.

Moira worked as an office manager for Karp, Gutman and Bell, a small but well-known and respected law firm in downtown Chicago. On Wednesdays, Bartlett and Moira met for lunch in a small cafe, between her office and the Federal Building. He referred vaguely to his work as government stuff, and stated he was unable to discuss the particulars with anyone, when asked.

Eventually, she quit quizzing him about work knowing his inability to answer. He had never been specific but Moira assumed he worked for a federal agency, maybe even the CIA. Bartlett traveled occasionally for weeks at a time but always kept in contact with her. She understood that part of his life was concealed.

Like Bartlett, Moira had no family in the city. She was from a small town in Iowa and had come to Chicago a decade earlier to begin a career. She was as alone as he. Most of her close family was either deceased or elderly, as was his. It seemed improbable that they had found each other and now he would have to temporarily leave her.

Following the shooting, Bartlett drove directly to Oak Street in downtown Chicago without encountering a cop or a squad car. He double parked the car and left the engine running. He emptied the glove box and removed the license plate. Then he walked to Michigan Avenue and took a cab to Evanston.

Upon his arrival at Moira's, Bartlett proceeded to her garage and retrieved a black satchel that he had hidden in the rafters. He started her old Volvo and backed it out into the driveway, and left the engine running and entered the house. Her scent was in the air. He realized how much he would miss her. After quickly packing some belongings, he took the pencil and paper next to the telephone and hurriedly wrote a short note.

Darling - I can't explain just now, but I have to leave for a while. My situation requires complete confidentiality. I won't be able to contact you and don't try to contact me. I don't expect you to understand, but I hope you'll try. When I can, I'll explain. I've taken your car. You'll find it in the long-term lot at O'Hare. I'll send the parking stub showing the exact location. There's parking money in the envelope. I love you more than I can tell you. Please try to understand...JB

The note, like all of his emotional exclamations, seemed inadequate. He placed a thick envelope under the note. It contained $5,000. Moira was the first beneficiary of Alderman Brezinski's death.

Chapter 5

Several hours after the execution of Alderman Brezinski, Bartlett was on a flight to New Orleans. He had two carry-on bags containing clothes and $50,000 in getaway cash which he had retrieved from Moira's garage. He would have to return to Chicago later to collect the rest of his money, which he had stashed in safety deposit boxes.

The alderman's death was significant news in Chicago. The killing was described as a mob-style execution, which meant the police had no clues to the identity of the killer, and suggested publicly that the killing was somehow justified.

Reporters discovered that Alderman Brezinski was either hated or feared, or both, by fellow politicians and business associates. There was a sincere lack of sympathy surrounding his death and the Chicago police seemed to feel that it was a murder that wouldn't be solved. The memorial services were poorly attended.

Detective David Coles, the Chicago Police Department's eyewitness, had seen the killer but didn't get a good look at him. It was believed the assassin was wearing a disguise. The license plate on the getaway car was stolen, and the car had not been found.

It was assumed by the authorities that the getaway car had been stolen, too, and was later disposed.

In New Orleans, Bartlett routinely read the Chicago newspapers at the public library. He was relieved by the lack of interest in the Brezinski story.

Within weeks, after a brief flurry of investigative reports, media interest in the shooting and Brezinski's corrupt career had quickly moved from the front to the inside pages of The Tribune.

But Bartlett couldn't forget the moment his eyes had met Coles' outside the restaurant.

*   *   *

Detective David Coles immediately recognized John Bartkowski. It was a face he'd never forget. Thirty-one years earlier, Bartkowski had saved his life in Vietnam.

Coles joined the Chicago police force after returning from Vietnam. Ex-military applicants were always welcome in the police department because of their training and combat experience. Coles was a tough, dedicated officer who moved quickly through the ranks.

He'd arrived in Vietnam as an inexperienced, untested second lieutenant and he relied heavily on his sergeant, the intense young soldier named Bartkowski. "You're either a natural-born soldier or a natural-born killer," Coles remembered telling him.

When he last saw Bartkowski, Coles was being loaded into a helicopter for transport to a field hospital. Their night patrol had walked into a Vietcong ambush. Coles was shot in both legs and believed he would bleed to death in the muddy field. He could still smell and taste the mud and grass and remember the chill as his life seeped away.

Bartkowski had appeared from nowhere. He cinched Coles' legs to stop the bleeding, administered morphine and then carried Coles several miles back to their base camp.

*   *   *

Coles had always hoped he would see Bartkowski again to properly thank him for saving his life. But years later and under these circumstances, Coles almost regretted seeing Bartkowski again.

However, after the killing, Coles was not surprised to be informed the Chicago police had been investigating Alderman Brezinski for some time. The facts were apparently well-known, but difficult to prove: Brezinski had received bribes related to a variety of enterprises in his district. He virtually controlled the permits required for construction and trash removal. City health and fire inspectors approved substandard conditions in the district in return for payoffs which were shared with Brezinski. He enjoyed cash, vodka and prostitutes, pretty much in that order and all together if possible.

Privately, Coles thought Bartkowski had done law enforcement and the city of Chicago a favor. And, for his own personal reasons, he felt justified enough to give Bartkowski a free pass.

Chapter 6

In New Orleans, Bartlett called on an old Army buddy, Benny Gentry, whom he hadn't seen in years. He discovered Gentry was still the gentle, stoned-out soul Bartlett remembered from Vietnam. Together they had operated a thriving, small-time black market sales enterprise during the war. Gentry welcomed Bartkowski to New Orleans as if he were a long-lost brother, and asked few questions about his sudden arrival.

Gentry, like Bartlett, had also found a profession in 'Nam: he was now handling shipments of cocaine and marijuana for a powerful Panamanian dealer named Hector Aguilar.

Aguilar's drugs were being brought to the States from South America aboard old, rusty freighters bound for New Orleans. Late at night, the ships would rendezvous with Gentry's tiny fleet of powerboats miles off the coast of Louisiana. The powerboats would load up the cargo and transport them to isolated spots in the bayous south of New Orleans. On shore, 10-man teams waited to offload the cargo into vans headed for Gentry's warehouse in Bridge City.

At the warehouse, the bundles would be opened and repackaged into smaller parcels and placed inside the body panels of late-model vehicles. Gentry hired transport haulers to take the vehicles from New Orleans to several used car lots in Detroit and Chicago. He frequently mentioned to Bartlett that marijuana was now worth more per pound than gold.

Bartlett recognized an opportunity for himself and, with Gentry's help, parlayed some of his cash into a small warehouse and a business he named SC Marketing. Gentry provided Bartlett with contacts and new identification.

Soon, Bartlett was "Emery Clements," owner and operator of SC Marketing, buying excess inventory from discount stores and warehouses, repackaging it and reselling it to Aguilar's retail contacts in the Caribbean and South America.

The profits on the repackaged goods were slim, but the cash, which he shipped out of the country for Aguilar with the repackaged merchandise, made SC Marketing an extremely lucrative venture for Bartlett. His work for Aguilar was fast and efficient, and there were no problems with U.S. Customs.

As he gained Aguilar's confidence, large amounts of cash were being shipped through SC Marketing. Clements had already shipped over $2 million of Aguilar's money.

Once a week Aguilar's drug money was delivered to Clements at his warehouse. Neatly bundled stacks of $50s and $100s were repackaged in boxes with clock radios, toasters and tape recorders and then shipped to Aguilar's contacts. Emery Clements was paid in cash 3 percent of the amount shipped. Benny Gentry received a consulting fee from this.

In six months, Bartlett had put away thousands of dollars from his business venture with Aguilar. The business and affiliation with Aguilar were risky and he was almost ready to close the operation and leave New Orleans. He knew that business relationships with men like Aguilar were temporary, at best.

A casual visit to St. Croix started Bartlett thinking about relocating there, and he began to secretly visit the island regularly. Soon he was planning a permanent move to St. Croix. His plans were hastened by the discovery that Adela Hammonds, an employee, had been stealing money from Aguilar's shipments.

On the recommendation of Gentry, Bartlett had hired Adela Hammonds to manage the routine business of SC Marketing. Gentry claimed she was trustworthy, loyal and would be totally cooperative. Bartlett always wondered if he could still trust Gentry, but decided he would find out for himself.

At first, Hammonds seemed exactly what Bartlett wanted: an efficient manager who didn't bother him with the details of the daily operations. The overt routines of SC Marketing were her responsibility. She seemed to be unaware of the specialized shipments which Bartlett handled personally.

But when returning early from an appointment one morning, Bartlett found her in his private office. Knowing he had locked the door, he saw a file cabinet was open and Adela was looking through a file folder on his desk.

Bartlett's thoughts raced, but he tried to maintain his composure. He could see she was surprised and frightened.

"I was looking through the Big-Mart file," she said nervously. "The guys in the warehouse needed to see a copy of their last shipment and I didn't have one." She blushed. *She was lying*. Bartlett wondered for a moment if she was an undercover police officer looking for evidence.

"I thought I told you that no one was to come in here," he said. He didn't mention the unlocked door.

"You did, but I couldn't find the Big-Mart file, and I thought you might have it here. I'm sorry. I didn't realize you'd be upset."

She was aware of the blackness in Bartlett's eyes and hoped he wouldn't immediately miss the money she had taken from the bag inside the cardboard box in the file cabinet. Perhaps the open Big-Mart file would distract him into thinking about her explanation, flimsy as it was, rather than the cash. She had taken $5,000 from several of the shipments in the past few months.

"I was trying to do my job... I didn't know how to get in touch with you..."

Bartlett could sense her fear.

"...I'm very sorry. It won't happen again. I was trying to help."

Bartlett glared at her. "We'll talk about it later," he said. "I need to work in here now."

After she left his office, Bartlett checked the latest shipment of cash. Regrettably for Adela, he discovered $5,000 was missing. *How much had she taken over time?* He wondered if Aguilar had noticed yet.

She has to be eliminated. I can't risk losing any more of Aguilar's cash. Aguilar will eventually miss the money and hold me responsible. She has left me no choice. There's no innocent explanation.

Later in the day, Bartlett asked Adela to make a reservation for himself on the night flight to Atlanta, telling her he'd be gone for a few days. He suggested they meet and talk about things after work. She seemed relieved to have an opportunity to talk. There had been a chilling silence in the office throughout the afternoon.

Bartlett listened as Adela locked the front door at five. A moment later, she knocked lightly on his office door and entered. She was uneasy, as if she knew that he had discovered the theft.

Adela Hammonds was a tall, full-bodied, blond-haired woman. She was probably attractive by conventional standards, but Bartlett was never interested in her personally. He knew nothing about her family or friends. She received no personal calls or visits in the office. But someone would miss her, probably sooner rather than later.

"Have a seat," he said, offering her a Styrofoam cup with a bit of coffee in it. She took the cup a little nervously.

"I want to make clear," he said, "that this office and the files in it...are private." For a moment, he hoped that there would be a response that would somehow commute her sentence.

"I...I understand and I'm sorry about this morning. I really was just trying to help...the guys wanted a copy of the last shipment and I...."

"Don't explain," Bartlett said. *She is lying.* "... I understand. I just want to be sure that we understand each other about this office. I'm a very private man."

He moved from behind the desk and stood beside Adela. Again he wished that she could somehow be forgiven and it would make it unnecessary for him to kill her. He only allowed himself a fleeting moment of remorse.

"I do understand," she said, "and ..."

"I thought you would," said Bartlett, moving behind her as he placed his hands on her shoulders. She was tense. Quickly, he covered her mouth and nose with his hand. *She mustn't scream.* With the other hand he seized her skull and twisted violently. Her neck snapped with a popping noise and she crumpled in her chair. He shoved the body onto the floor and arranged it in the fetal position so it would be easier to handle after rigor mortis set in.

She was probably stealing for herself, but she might have been working with Gentry. Perhaps even Aguilar. He was sure there were people who wanted to know more about Emery Clements and SC Marketing.

"Poor thing," he said over the body as a kind of last rite.

Bartlett made his decision quickly. He opened Aguilar's latest shipment and placed as much cash as he could get into his briefcase: approximately $195,000. There wasn't time to count.

He moved Adela's body into the warehouse and placed it on top of an empty skid. He doused the body, a small amount of the remaining cash and the skid with gasoline. Then he poured more gasoline over the stacked rows of cardboard boxes. This would be the end of Adela Hammonds, Emery Clements and SC Marketing. He knew Aguilar would begin to search for him immediately.

He was confident there were no visible connections between Emery Clements, SC Marketing and Jim Bartlett, who was about to begin a new life in St. Croix. Gentry would have to take care of himself.

He scarcely looked back at the SC Marketing warehouse as it exploded in flames.

* * *

A day later the *Times-Picayune* ran a lead story about the fire, the body and some burnt cash discovered in the ruins. Arson was the presumed cause. The unidentified body was believed to be Adela Hammonds, the office manager who was missing. The police were searching for her next-of-kin. Law enforcement had been unable to locate Emery Clements, the owner of the business, although it was believed he had gone to Atlanta the night of the fire. The authorities wanted to talk to him.

Bartlett also noticed a small article about a local businessman, Benjamin Gentry, who had been beaten to death.

Detective Henry Toussaint, the lead detective for the New Orleans police department, wasn't able to retrieve much evidence of value from the smoldering ruins of SC Marketing. A hint of blackened cash, the body and a few charred electronics were about all that remained. Not surprisingly, he found burnt fragments from more than a dozen travel brochures inside the building.

Chapter 7

Bartlett, reassured again that Aguilar hadn't located him on the island, looked out the bedroom window and momentarily gazed down upon the shore road, the beach and the ocean.

He entered the bathroom and examined himself in the mirror: a very fit, young looking 51-year-old man, 6 feet tall and tanned. He was dark-haired and sporadically liked the shaved head look. He was proud of his appearance. His weight hadn't varied 10 pounds in 25 years, but he was aware of a gradual loss of strength and muscle tone. Regrettable, but inevitable. Nevertheless, he was in good physical condition and he was still ready for combat.

He was aware of his own musky odor as he stepped into the shower, an odor he associated with perspiration and sex. The thought of somehow having sex with Denise Spangler again quickly aroused him. He would call her.

Still, Bartlett felt love for Moira, but months ago, out of loneliness, he had decided to date again. He had no idea whether or not Moira would be back in his life. Denise had become a person whom he had relied on only for sex.

His shower was brief. Fresh water was always a concern on the island. He imagined containers for collecting and storing time, like the cisterns for water under the house. He didn't want to run out of either.

He had watched the modest three-bedroom home that he ultimately bought gradually emerge on the hillside above the coastal highway. He occasionally stopped to talk to the workmen and observe their progress. He envied the simplicity of their work.

He introduced himself to the designer and builder, Peter Van Hout, who enthusiastically showed Bartlett the plans for the house. "One of the best on the island," Van Hout told him.

When Bartlett learned that Van Hout's client was backing out of their deal, he bought the house for $300,000 in cash.

Now he complimented himself for choosing the sturdy, well-designed concrete structure. Fresh water and electricity were precious commodities on St. Croix and he was well supplied with both. A backup gas generator was ready in the shed behind the house and the cisterns were always fully filled. When the perimeter security system was complete, Bartlett would have a tight, independent little fortress on the hillside above the sea. He had envisioned someday being able to retire here with Moira, but he didn't know if that would ever materialize or not.

The scale and simplicity of life on St. Croix appealed to Bartlett as did the beautiful tropical landscapes. Some of the landscapes in St. Croix were very similar to what he had first encountered in Vietnam. Only in Vietnam, it was mingled with the sights and sounds of war and death. Often he had tried to imagine an idyllic Vietnam without the war, without the young dead.

In St. Croix, the simplicity of life and peacefulness seemed natural and continuous. In Vietnam, the only peacefulness he had experienced was through drug and alcohol abuse in the bars and brothels of Saigon. It was a normal alternative to the seemingly endless conflict.

On St. Croix, he had never been so relaxed. He took long, slow walks on the beach below his house and occasionally traveled to nearby Buck Island National Park. He used scuba gear there to lazily explore the teeming aquatic life of the reef. At first, he imagined himself bringing Moira there on the long lazy afternoons he had planned for their future. It seemed improbable now that Moira would ever join him.

At night, he enjoyed Christiansted and the slow dance-like rhythms of the old town; an old lady during the day, an old whore at night. He'd spend plenty of time there, too.

Bartlett was ready to retire from the business. He believed he could plan his exit as carefully as he had planned his assignments; a few more and he would have the money he needed. He could retire and on his own terms. He had accumulated more than $1,250,000 in his Cayman bank account, which would allow him to live comfortably for many years. The property on St. Croix was worth close to $400,000 and he had a large stash of ready cash.

With more than $1 million properly invested along with profits from a gift shop he owned, he could live an anonymous, simple and comfortable life on St. Croix.

There was a certain irony associated with his double life. On the island, he was the friendly, slightly aloof, proprietor of a touristy gift store. Away from the island, he was an anonymous professional killer.

He glanced at the clock. It was 8:30. He would have to hurry if he was going to reach the Ursula Shop before 9. He liked to be there when Rosa arrived. He shaved and dressed, careful as always about his appearance.

Bartlett splashed some spiced cologne on his face and put on his watch and ring. Moira had given him the cologne and the sight of the bottle reminded him of her.

Chapter 8

Bartlett departed for the shop, turning his Jeep east onto the shore road toward the inlet on Salt River Bay. He had to make a conscious effort to drive in the left lane as the law on the island required, particularly after returning from mainland trips. Sometimes he would get confused and forget, but quickly he would be reminded by the honking of an oncoming vehicle.

Most of the island roads were curved, old and narrow. But, the newer highway connecting the towns of Christiansted and Frederiksted slashed like a fresh scar across the landscape.

The crowded housing projects and rickety shacks on the road through Christiansted reminded him of his childhood ethnic neighborhood in Chicago, where families were crowded into tiny apartments on Division Street. He remembered vividly the noise of crying and screaming children and adults, typical for everyday living in the building. And he remembered the wonderful scents in the staircase of freshly baked breads and a wide variety of meals being prepared in the nine-story apartment building.

On the hottest summer days, the pungent stench of some of the other apartments would be noticeable in his bedroom. So in the evenings, he would ascend to the rooftop to take advantage of fresh air and an occasional cool breeze off Lake Michigan. He remembered his resentment of the comfortable people in their air-conditioned houses farther north in the city. He had traveled quite a distance.

He believed he understood how the islanders felt about the elaborate houses and residents along the coast, and the invisible fences surrounding them. It surprised him there weren't more burglaries or violence on the island.

The shops lining the roadway into town were small and shabby. Here and there an American chain store appeared, conspicuously new-looking like a tourist unaccustomed to the sun and salt air.

Bartlett pulled into the parking lot of the Athena Shopping Center, a group of little shops popular with the locals. He especially liked the grocery store coffee, served at the small "to go" counter in the rear.

"Large regular?" asked the lanky young man from behind the counter who frequently served Bartlett.

"Yes, thanks," said Bartlett, handing him $3. "I'll take a paper, too."

He picked up a copy of The Avis, the local newspaper, from a small stack on the counter. He began scanning the headlines on the top fold of the front page.

He climbed back into the Jeep with paper and coffee in hand. He again took a look at the paper and, in the lower right-hand corner under the fold, was the story Bartlett had been expecting to see. "LOCAL MAN KILLED IN ACCIDENT," read the headline.

According to the account, John Strawberry, 29, died in a "vehicular accident" on the northern part of the island near Cane Bay. A jogger had reported finding the wreck and the remains along the rocky shoreline. Police believed Strawberry had been drinking and had lost control of his moped. The story stated the young man had apparently fallen to his death from high atop the curvy and treacherous north shore road.

Bartlett regretted killing Strawberry, but he had no choice. Strawberry made a very bad decision. Bartlett was relieved the death was being treated as an accident. It wasn't the first time he had felt such relief.

He finished his coffee and was ready for another when he reached Company Street. The Ursula Shop occupied one of the weathered old stucco buildings which lined the street not far from Fort Christiansted and the old waterfront. Henry's and Tutu John's were nearby. *Strawberry had probably spent his last hours, and last dollars, in one of them.*

He decided to name the store "The Ursula Shop" after reading in a tourism brochure about Saint Ursula, to whom Christopher Columbus had dedicated the Virgin

Islands, now a United States territory. Years earlier, the shop was one of the many buildings damaged by Hurricane Hugo. My employers in the mob would be amused if they knew I owned a pink stucco gift shop, he imagined.

Bartlett had signed a multiple-year lease on the property and hired Van Hout to supervise the remodeling. He hoped it could withstand another hurricane with minimum damage.

Upon his arrival behind the Ursula Shop, he parked and unlocked the security grate and door and entered the shop. He deactivated the alarm system and made a pot of coffee.

The shelves and counters were stocked with souvenirs, postcards, sunglasses, shorts, T-shirts, beach sandals, oils and lotions supplied by a Miami wholesaler. In addition, there was a nice selection of picture frames, jewelry and crafts created mainly from driftwood and shells, handmade by the locals.

Rosa Rodriguez managed the shop for Bartlett, and would arrive in a few minutes. She had come to St. Croix from Puerto Rico a few years earlier with her husband Juan, a minor player in the local drug trade. He had disappeared after trying to rip off his supplier.

Bartlett liked and trusted Rosa. She spoke English and Spanish fluently, and enough French, when required, to make herself understood. She was devoted to the shop and the regular paychecks from Bartlett.

She was the center of a group of friends who lived in Frederiksted and sometimes visited her in the shop. Bartlett knew she sent money to her family in Puerto Rico, and he was not unaware of the complications involved if she became a threat. But he foresaw no difficulties for Rosa in the shop. There was nothing in its operation that could compromise his stateside career.

The shop served Bartlett's needs, and it provided an ample supplemental income. Mostly, though, it was a secure and anonymous cover for Bartlett. He was grateful he hadn't encountered any familiar faces from Chicago or New Orleans in the shop or during his infrequent buying trips to Miami.

"Emery Clements" seemed to have disappeared entirely, and the fire and murder at SC Marketing were nearly forgotten by most, except Aguilar and the New Orleans police department.

Through a confidential source, Bartlett had learned Aguilar had offered $100,000 to anyone who would lead him to Emery Clements. Aguilar would be relentless in his search and he would never forget about the loss of his money and being double-crossed by Clements.

As usual, first thing every Monday morning Bartlett picked up the phone and called his Chicago answering service. The service said there was an urgent message for him to call Frank Russo. It was highly unusual to receive a message requesting a callback to Russo.

Messages usually meant Bartlett would be getting an assignment from one of the mob bosses. A request to contact Russo meant something else. *There was a problem.*

Chapter 9

Franklin Delano Russo managed the tiny one-room office of JBS Personnel Services on the top floor of the Kenilworth building, just as he had before Bartlett's departure from Chicago. He was fond of slick, shiny double-breasted suits, which he bought two at a time from an outlet store. Cheap, uncomfortable imported loafers completed his ensemble, and he was seldom without a gigantic Guatemalan cigar. Although he never carried a gun, he always wore his shoulder holster. The neighborhood juveniles made fun of him, nicknaming him "FDR," which unbeknownst to him meant in their jargon "fuckin' dumbass runt." When Bartlett first met him, he thought the huge cigar might set the little man in the peculiar suit on fire.

Arriving at the office about 11 each morning, Russo first checked for messages, then leafed through a stack of old *Hustlers* and *Playboys* while he smoked the noxious cigars.

Russo had been recommended to Bartlett as loyal,

discreet and a bit slow. He had worked for the Tomasello crime family, occasionally delivering pizzas and sandwiches for "Big Eddie" Salimento at his pizzeria. Salimento was a distant cousin of Anthony Tomasello, a well-known Chicago underboss. Russo was proud of his connections and thankful for the job with JBS.

His responsibilities to Bartlett were simple: relay phone messages to the number Bartlett provided and take care of office expenses. Bartlett never visited the office and it didn't surprise Russo when he heard Bartlett's message announcing another telephone number change.

Russo received a monthly bank check from an anonymous off-shore account, from which he was to pay the office expenses and himself. For Russo, it was a good job, and his girlfriend didn't know about the office charges he racked up on the 900 numbers. The checks now were coming from a Swiss bank in the Cayman Islands. Russo thought he would like to visit there one day. He pictured himself in a flashy, lightweight suit sipping pina coladas surrounded by bikinied women on a secluded beach in the Caribbean.

Bartlett's initial instructions to Russo were: talk to no one about the arrangements, never use a cell phone and never call unless there was a message. Bartlett had worn a disguise during his only meeting with Russo, and doubted that Russo could identify him.

Bartlett utilized two different professional answering service firms. His clients were given one of those numbers where they could contact him. That number never needed to be changed. And, Russo was given both numbers to receive and relay client messages to Bartlett. Russo had been instructed to call the one service for messages and relay them to Bartlett using the other service.

Upon receipt of a new message from Russo, Bartlett would contact the caller, discuss the details of the job and accept or reject the assignment. Bartlett would generally accept most of the offers unless there was a really valid reason not to. Mob bosses don't like being told "no" when they ask someone to do a service for them.

The assignment terms were simple. As soon as Bartlett accepted a job, a deposit representing half the fee needed to be in his Cayman bank account before he would begin preparing, with balance due on completion. To date, he had never left an assignment incomplete. It wouldn't be wise for him to do so.

Most of his assignments came from the heads of the New York crime families, their national affiliates and some other special referrals they provided. He chose his jobs and his clients carefully and he wouldn't take a job unless all of his conditions were met, including absolute anonymity for himself. He knew he couldn't be too careful about concealing his location and his identity.

He planned the hits meticulously and he was proud of his professionalism. Upon request, and for more money, he could make the murders appear to be accidental. He was reputed to be "the best" and he was exceptionally well paid.

Street hoods could get up to $5,000 per hit. Bartlett's minimum was $25,000, the fee based on the difficulty of the work and the profile of the target.

Sometimes months passed between calls and assignments and Bartlett welcomed the silence, knowing new clients would contact him when they were in need. After almost 28 years, he had maintained a solid reputation and had many satisfied customers.

Chapter 10

It was almost 9:00 when Bartlett checked his watch; Rosa would arrive at any moment. She opened the shop promptly at 9:00 and closed promptly at 5:00. Bartlett appreciated her punctuality. He heard her opening the front door as he poured himself another cup of coffee.

"Good morning, Rosa."

"Good morning," she replied.

Rosa was a good-looking, dark-complected woman with fine features. Her black hair fell to her shoulders in elaborate French braids. She was slender and full breasted, a combination which Bartlett found nearly irresistible. Rosa dressed simply and comfortably, usually in a skimpy cotton shift. He enjoyed watching her move through the shop, and he enjoyed the scent of her perfume, which often lingered after she had gone. Frequently, Bartlett found himself wondering what it would be like to wake up next to her.

"How was the trip in?" Bartlett asked, referring to the

ride from Frederiksted.

"OK," she answered quietly. The normally vivacious Rosa was subdued.

"Will you please clean the entryway today? It really needs it."

"Sure," she said quietly.

Bartlett watched Rosa with some concern. Her present demeanor was unlike her.

"Rosa, is everything all right?"

"Oh, Mr. Bartlett, it's not me, it's my friend Juliet. We ride to town together in the morning. Her brother died this weekend."

"I'm sorry. What happened?"

"He was partying in town, at Henry's, and he drank too much and drove off the cliff on the north shore road, just past Cane's Bay. You know, on the curvy stretch, several miles past your house. I feel so bad for Juliet and for her brother. He was just a young man."

"Would you like some time off to be with your friend, with Juliet?" asked Bartlett, uncomfortably.

"No thank you, but I would like a few hours on Wednesday to go to the funeral."

"Sure that's fine…I'm very sorry."

"Thank you, Mr. Bartlett. I'll clean the entryway now. Should I make coffee?"

"I already did. Will you please go to the bank? We need some money for the cash register. Take a $100 bill…that should be enough to start."

"Alright, after I finish the entryway," she said.

Rosa was touched by Bartlett's consideration. She sometimes wondered what it would be like to be with him, too.

Bartlett watched as she grabbed the $100 bill, the bank bag and headed out the door. He was glad to have a few minutes alone in the shop. Her news had given him an unusual feeling of guilt and he was concerned about the message from Russo.

* * *

Officer Marcus Caulier strolled into the Ursula Shop moments after Rosa left. He often dropped in to browse and flirt with Rosa, but now he approached Bartlett directly. Today, Officer Caulier obviously believed in the solemn importance of his uniform.

"Mr. Bartlett?" he asked, officiously.

"Yes…"

Officer Caulier's lazy left eye wandered left to right as he talked. Bartlett found it difficult to look directly into his face.

The officer held up a driver's license with a tiny ID

photo. It was Strawberry.

"Do you know this man?"

Bartlett squinted at the picture and tried not to let his recognition show.

"I don't believe I do. Why?"

"He died this weekend, in an accident near Cane's Bay. We found some letters addressed to you on his person..."

The officer produced four damaged envelopes addressed to Bartlett.

"Do you know how he might have gotten them?"

"I have no idea," Bartlett said.

"He might have taken them from your mailbox...he was not particular about ownership. Might they have been in your mailbox on Saturday, Mr. Bartlett?"

"They could have been," said Bartlett.

"Well, I'll give them back to you," said the officer.

"How did he die?" asked Bartlett.

"He drove off the north shore road on his scooter and broke his neck. He was probably drunk. Perhaps he robbed your mailbox just before...."

"Perhaps he did..." said Bartlett, accepting the letters. "Thank you for these...too bad about the young man."

"Yes, he was careless. Very bad to be careless."

"Apparently so," said Bartlett.

"One more thing," said Officer Caulier. "Do you smoke marijuana?"

"No," said Bartlett. "Why?"

"Apparently Mr. Strawberry did. Good day."

Rosa entered the shop as the officer was leaving. He smiled at her as he left.

"Is everything all right?" she asked Bartlett.

"Yeah. Some kids have been stealing mail on the north shore road. The officer returned some letters to me. Nothing to worry about."

"I hope not," said Rosa.

"No, just petty larceny." Nothing to worry about.

Chapter 11

Detective Toussaint kept the file on SC Marketing on top of his pile of cases. There were only shreds of evidence to review concerning the arson and murder investigation. Adela Hammonds was deceased, Benjamin Gentry was deceased and the main suspect, Emory Clements, was missing without a trace.

There were no fingerprints lifted from Clements' furnished, south-side apartment. It had been wiped clean. There were no personal possessions left inside either. DNA samples were taken from hair follicles found in the furniture and drains in the bathroom. They were being processed by the crime lab. His late-model Ford sedan, found abandoned in the airport parking garage, was licensed and titled under SC Marketing. The auto was clean, too. It had been purchased from Gentry for cash.

There was reason to believe Clements had taken a flight to Atlanta after the fire, because Hammonds had commented to one of the warehouse employees that the boss was headed to Atlanta. However, Clements' name did not appear on any outgoing flight passenger lists. Toussaint doubted if he had taken any flight to Atlanta.

There were no known photographs or records on Clements anywhere. Toussaint discovered Clements was a very private person, with the exception of his business relationship with Hammonds. Toussaint surmised Clements had some kind of a business association with Gentry, too.

The immigrants, who worked at the SC Marketing warehouse, could barely speak English and were not very helpful. They had been paid weekly in cash. After the fire and murder, they were scared and apprehensive about talking with the police. Most of them were illegals and had mainly dealt with Hammonds on a regular basis, instead of Bartlett.

All of Clements' personal bills, including the apartment, had been paid by certified bank checks, payer being Adela Hammonds, office manager, SC Marketing.

Vendors, who dealt with SC Marketing, were not helpful either. All business dealings with SC Marketing were done by phone with Hammonds and they were paid COD for the goods and services they provided.

Clements never ate out much or made personal contacts. Toussaint couldn't find anyone who had either met or who had an association with Clements or who could or would help to identify him. No doubt Clements had met Aguilar at some time through Gentry, but Aguilar would not discuss anything about his operations, including Clements, with the police.

The apartment leasing company hadn't kept many records, other than the rental contract and copies of the monthly rental receipts. Clements was rarely noticed by anyone at the obscure apartment complex. Residents described him as a white male, average height and weight with short dark hair.

The whereabouts of Emery Clements, before or after his brief appearance in New Orleans, seemed impossible to determine. It was as if he had never existed.

The search of Adela Hammonds' one-room efficiency apartment was interesting but puzzling. Early in the investigation, Toussaint had been able to determine Hammonds was using a false identity and her real name was Adela Curtin.

She was 35, single, an orphan and a little-known private detective from Baton Rouge, La. Apparently she had come to New Orleans "on the job" and she had made no friends in the area. Her employer was unknown.

The day of her murder, someone had broken into her apartment and hurriedly searched through her possessions, which were scattered about the room.

Toussaint conducted a thorough search of her room looking for clues. He found personal items, clothes, books, a small tape recording device minus the cassette tapes and some blank notepads and pens.

Taped to the bottom of one of her clothes drawers was a manila envelope. Inside, there was a bank book showing a $27,725 balance and a month-old deposit ticket for $5,000, along with $2,000 in cash. Curtin's professional P.I. credentials were inside the envelope, too.

The person who had ransacked the room had overlooked an impression of some words left on a blank notepad, near the phone. A police technician discovered them by lightly drawing over the pad with a soft lead pencil, revealing the names of Bartkowski, Gentry and Aguilar. A phone number and the words "dep in Carib" were on the top page. Curtin appeared to have been interested in Clements, but she had left few clues.

When Toussaint dialed the phone number on the pad, he reached an answering service in Chicago. He'd left a message but they didn't return his call. When he checked back a few hours later, the operator informed him that the company serviced thousands of clients. After searching their client lists for Hammonds, Curtin, Bartkowski or Clements, the service operator was unable to come up with a match.

Toussaint presumed that SC Marketing was a trans-shipping operation for Aguilar's drug cash. Adela Curtin probably died because of this knowledge and maybe for skimming money. He wondered who she had been working for.

Detective Toussaint noticed his income was negatively affected after SC Marketing went up in flames. He had regularly collected cash from the fringes of Aguilar's operation. Benny Gentry had always been good for a $1,000 a month. Evidently, SC Marketing had been more important to Aguilars' operation than Toussaint had previously suspected.

Toussaint knew Aguilar was responsible for Gentry's death but he couldn't prove it. A police informant claimed he had been told Aguilar had gone half-crazy when he learned about the SC Marketing fire. Reportedly, Aguilar's people had been extraordinarily brutal to Gentry when they interrogated him concerning Clements whereabouts. His body was discovered in an abandoned waterfront warehouse. The murder weapon, found next to Gentry's battered remains, was a Louisville Slugger. *Benny Gentry endured a terrible death.*

According to the informant, one of the things he had heard Gentry revealed about Clements was Clements' real name was Bartkowski. Before being beaten to death, Gentry said Bartkowski was a Vietnam veteran and had lived in Chicago. Benny was either very brave or that was all he knew about Emery Clements.

Toussaint knew Aguilar wouldn't rest until Emery Clements was found and Toussaint intended to collect the reward he had heard Aguilar was offering. *Clements or Bartkowski or whomever is probably long gone by now.*

Chapter 12

The Kalamazoo River glides between the resort towns of Saugatuck and Douglas, Mich., just before it empties into Lake Michigan. Sheltered by dunes, hills and patches of the old oak forest, the two towns have been popular as summer resorts for more than a hundred years. The impressive Victorian summer houses along the lake and river are proud symbols of wealth, old and new.

In one of these, a rambling, tall, gray-frame structure, perched on a bluff overlooking the lake, State Sen. Louis Stroh stepped out of the shower and began drying himself. He had been coming to the "The Cottage" for nearly 50 years, and sometimes he thought he could still hear the voices from summers past. His grandfather, who made a fortune during the last years of the lumber boom in Michigan, had built the cottage. The Stroh family had enjoyed a prominent position in Michigan business and political circles for decades. Stroh had spent summers here as a child; his wife and children had spent summers here; and now he was alone here with Anne.

The nervous buzzing of the bedroom phone startled him. Only the office secretary knew they were going to the cottage. Louis wanted these trips to be quiet and romantic times with Anne. He listened as she answered the phone. Stroh was ready to get back into bed and resume their lovemaking.

A moment later Anne Bishop appeared in the bathroom doorway. She was wearing only brief cotton panties. Her body, round, full and feminine, always excited him; she made him feel 30 years younger and he was proud to be with her. He hoped it would always be so.

"Who was it?" he asked.

"Henry Wallace. I told him you'd call back. He said you had his number. He told me it was a personal matter. Do I know him?"

Anne noticed the brief look of alarm that passed over Stroh's face.

"You haven't met him. I'll call him in a while."

"Who is he?" asked Anne.

"He's a lawyer in Detroit. He probably wants to know about the casino bill. I've known him for years. He represents a group of family businesses in Detroit and they think they can make some money on the new casinos. I don't know why he's calling me here. He could have left a message at the office."

Stroh was amused by the thought of the lovely, nearly naked Anne taking a message in bed from the self-important Henry Wallace. But the probable reason for the call made him uncomfortable.

Louis pulled Anne close to him and hugged her. Her skin was wonderfully smooth. He could feel her nipples firmly against him. He wondered if she knew how much pleasure she gave him. But the phone call from Wallace seemed to interrupt their romantic mood.

"Everything all right?" Anne asked.

"Yeah, everything's fine."

Anne noted the characteristic slight tremor of the lower lip that Stroh exhibited when he was lying. She wondered how many others had noticed it, too.

"Would you like some breakfast?" she asked. "I think there are some eggs and sausage in the fridge."

"That would be nice."

Stroh watched as she slipped on a brassiere and a T-shirt. He enjoyed watching her as much as he enjoyed touching her. Anne was full of unexpected little graces and dance-like movements that fascinated him. He wondered how and when she had learned them.

Anne paused in front of the mirror and quickly brushed her hair and applied rouge and lipstick. She was proud of her appearance. It had been her passport since she had been a teenager. And it had brought her to this lovely cottage on a bluff overlooking Lake Michigan with this handsome older man from a wealthy family, who was also the majority leader of the state Senate.

Three years earlier, on the strength of an introduction from Christine Cass, Anne Bishop had gone to work in Stroh's office as an administrative assistant. As Christine predicted, Stroh had shown an immediate interest in her, but she had managed the relationship carefully. She didn't want to become one of Stroh's discarded romantic projects. After the sudden and unexpected death of Stroh's wife two years earlier, she had opened to him first as a friend and soon after as a lover. They had been inseparable during the past year and he was beginning to talk about marriage.

"I'll get dressed and be down in a minute," said Stroh as Anne walked out of the room. "Keep it warm for me."

Anne turned and smiled.

Within seconds, Stroh had found Wallace's number, grabbed the telephone and closed the bathroom door behind himself.

In Detroit, an answering machine responded in Wallace's office. As Stroh was leaving his name, Wallace picked up the phone.

"Thanks for calling back right away. I thought you might be out on your boat."

"Well, I'd like to be. What's up?" Stroh was aware of the anxiety in his own voice.

"Mr. Ricci needs to know how the casino legislation is going. He's concerned."

Stroh paused before he answered. "Tell him I'm doing

all I can, but there isn't the support I thought there'd be..."

"That's what Mr. Ricci paid you for, to find the support..."

"Look Wallace, you know how this works...I can't force this thing."

"We just want you to honor your agreement."

"I told you I'd give him his money back."

"We've talked about this … he doesn't want his money back. He wants the casino business. We've waited more than a year for you to deliver and Mr. Ricci is very, very anxious. If I were you, I'd get this taken care of as soon as possible."

Stroh paused. "What's that supposed to mean? Is that a threat?"

"You're an intelligent man. Don't ask me to interpret for you. By the way, Stroh, as I'm sure you know, none of this is personal. I represent Mr. Ricci. Was that Anne that answered the phone? She's a beautiful woman."

"I didn't think you'd met her..."

"I haven't. Keep me informed. I'll talk to you later."

Wallace hung up before Stroh could respond.

Stroh slammed the receiver down.

"Fuck!" he said.

On the eve of Stroh's election as Senate majority leader two years earlier, Wallace had approached him on behalf of Dominic Ricci. Ricci was the recognized head of organized crime in Detroit. He controlled a variety of businesses, legal and illegal, in southeastern Michigan. He was interested in the pending legislation that would allow casino gambling in downtown Detroit. Ricci wanted to substantially participate with a private investment group, who would operate the casinos.

Stroh knew that direct contact with Ricci would be political suicide, but Henry Wallace was a respected fixture on the legal and legislative scenes. Stroh hadn't known about his connection with Ricci. Apparently few did. Wallace arranged for a large but legal contribution to Stroh's re-election campaign. He also arranged a cash loan of $100,000 from Ricci to Stroh, to be forgiven when the casino legislation was passed.

With Stroh's assistance, Wallace made a series of private agreements with an investment group involved in the proposed casinos. But, despite the enthusiasm in Detroit for such a project, the governor and much of the Legislature were unexpectedly cool to the proposal. Stroh pushed as much as he dared but the legislation was nowhere near approval. He had worked hard and campaigned hard, both in and out of the state Senate, during 20 years in office to gain his current position. His leadership and re-election were threatened by difficulties with the casino legislation.

He now regretted the deal with Wallace and Ricci. Earlier, the casino legislation seemed like a sure thing and Stroh desperately needed Ricci's money. The family trust allowance Stroh received was smaller than most people imagined and he was accustomed to an expensive lifestyle.

The death benefit from his wife's insurance policy had replenished Stroh's resources. If Gina had lived, she would have divorced him, and the division of property and alimony payments would have ruined him. She would have been disappointed that he wasn't ruined. She would have been furious that Anne had moved so easily into the summer house and his life. She would have made disparaging remarks about his latest bimbo and his vain efforts to recapture his youthfulness.

But she was gone, killed instantly when she drove into the back end of a salt truck during a snowstorm. She was on her way to Grand Rapids to meet with her attorney.

Stroh searched nervously for a way to handle Wallace and Ricci.

Anne was serving the sausage and eggs when Stroh entered the kitchen. Her legs were tanned and lovely, and the white crescents of her buttocks showed beneath her T-shirt. He wanted to forget everything else and spend the day with her. Days at the cottage with Anne were rejuvenating for him; he felt as happy as he had during those endless summer days he spent at the cottage as a teenager.

After breakfast, they took coffee out onto the long porch. On the horizon was the sail of a small boat. Lake Michigan seemed calm and benign and Stroh remembered the first time he and his father had sailed across the lake. Saugatuck had become much more crowded recently, but Stroh enjoyed the crowds and the number of people who recognized him. Some of his wealthiest constituents visited him here. He enjoyed taking them out on his boat.

Stroh was well known and popular. His support for gay rights in the neighboring community of Douglas hadn't hurt him in Saugatuck or Lansing, although the Grand Rapids Christian Coalition denounced him.

After the second cup of coffee and the unusually short chat, Stroh arose from his chair and announced his intention to work on the boat. Anne knew the phone call had disturbed him and this was his way of sorting things out.

"How long will you be?" she asked.

"Not too long, darling. What say we rendezvous at the slip around 2, take a little cruise on the lake, and then go to The Yacht Club for dinner?" he asked.

"Fine," she said.

She understood his need to be alone. When he was ready, he would discuss things with her.

Stroh was oblivious to the picturesque drive down Lake View and along the river to the marina. The phone call from Wallace worried him. Ricci frightened him. There was little he could do about the legislation at this point. He had used up most of his favors in the Senate, and the mood in the Legislature was decidedly anti-gambling.

He could only tell Wallace and Ricci to wait. He was in a position now to return the $100,000 to Ricci. Ricci would understand; he was a businessman.

By the time he arrived at the marina, Stroh was determined to end the arrangement with Wallace and Ricci. He would muster the courage to tell Wallace their deal was off and return Ricci's money.

They would have to accommodate him. What else could they do? He was relieved that he had made the decision.

In his office in Detroit, Henry Wallace thought about his conversation with Stroh and then picked up the phone and placed another call.

A terse voice answered, "Army-Navy Surplus."

"This is Wallace. Please have Mr. Ricci call me."

"There's no Ricci here," the voice answered and hung up.

Wallace waited for Ricci's call.

Moments later his phone rang and Wallace let the machine answer.

"It's Ricci. Pick up the fuckin' phone." Ricci's voice and attitude were always unmistakable. He was an intelligent, educated man, but he spoke like he was auditioning for a low-budget gangster film.

Wallace picked up the phone.

"I talked to him. He's in Saugatuck with the woman. I

don't think he can pass the legislation, at least not this session. He asks you to be patient and he offered again to return the money."

"I don't want the fuckin' money. I want the casino in Greektown. You're gonna have to talk to him again, counselor. When you made this deal you assured me there was no problem. Goddamn politicians. Give them money for their campaigns, help them get elected, help them personally and suddenly they can't do anything for you. I want you to go over there and talk to your politician buddy, now. I'm tired of waiting. I don't want to wait for the next legislature or the next governor or the next any other fuckin' thing. Tell him I want this done right away. Do you understand me Wallace?"

"The political realities are such..."

"I don't give a shit. That's not what I want to hear from you. Go over and talk to your boy. Tell him again how serious I am. Ask him how much he likes whatshername that he's been screwin'. Tell him I want this thing done. And then call me back. Got it?"

"I'll do it right away," said Wallace.

Wallace decided to wait to call Stroh until after lunch. Waiting would give him some time to think about what he would say to Stroh and handle some arrangements for their meeting.

He didn't know if Stroh could get the bill passed, even with the motivation of a threat. And he didn't know how serious a warning Ricci really wanted Stroh to receive.

Ricci would be really upset if he were crossed again. He thought Ricci certainly wouldn't have a prominent politician killed, especially if he could be looked to for long-term favors. But if the legislation didn't materialize again in the next session, he wondered how Ricci would respond and if Ricci would hold him accountable for its failure.

Ricci was a clever but unpredictable businessman. His father, Carmine, had gotten his start bootlegging in Detroit during the Depression and had built a small empire. Carmine had been ruthless at the beginning of his career, benign at the end. Dominic Ricci had shown traces of his father's early ruthlessness when he had taken over the family businesses. His decision to eliminate rival gang members and consolidate power in his own family gained him immediate respect.

Wallace knew that his role was to get results for Ricci and, up until now, he had always been successful. There were consequences for those who failed Ricci. He would take Ricci's corporate plane to Saugatuck that evening and work on Stroh. He had no desire to test Ricci's resolve. Stroh could pick him up at the small municipal airport near Holland.

He looked forward to meeting Stroh's younger girlfriend, Anne, in person.

* * *

Stroh bought the "Summer Breeze," a 38-foot Morgan sloop, shortly after he received the $1.5 million settlement from his wife's insurance policy. It was his refuge of choice when he needed time alone.

He climbed on board, unlocked the hatch and stepped down into the cabin. The air was thick and still. He opened a teak cabinet and pulled out a bottle of scotch and a glass and poured himself a stiff drink.

I will return the money and that will be the end of it. Wallace will make it difficult, but there really is no alternative at this point. What would Ricci do? Sue me? The scotch soothed him.

The alcohol and humidity made Stroh sleepy. He lay down in the master cabin on the narrow bunk and was quickly asleep.

Anne's voice awoke him a couple of hours later. "Louis," she said. "Honey, wake up."

Stroh struggled to awaken. He was half asleep and half drunk.

"Louis, Wallace called again. He's coming to see you tonight. He wants you to pick him up at the Holland airport at 8. He said it's important. Is there something going on that I should know about?"

"No, dear. It's just some unfinished business. Wallace thinks he can pressure me on the casino bill, but he can't. It's just as well that we get this over with. I'll pick him up, take him to dinner and put him back on his plane. I'm sorry to spoil our evening ... we'll do something after I get rid of him."

Anne was confused and slightly hurt. Usually she was included in his business meetings.

Stroh struggled again to find the resolve he had felt earlier. *I am going to end the association with Ricci and Wallace tonight. I don't need them any longer, and, after I give Wallace the $100,000 personal check, my business with them will be concluded.*

Chapter 13

Wallace arrived at Ricci's private hangar and climbed aboard the shiny, twin-engine Cessna. The air-conditioned cabin was comfortably cool.

The pilot, Zane Whitney, closed and locked the hatch behind him. Whitney was the newest and youngest of Ricci's pilots. Wallace almost preferred a commercial flight where the pilot and his activities were unseen.

When Whitney offered a drink, Wallace opted for a stiff gin and tonic. He flew frequently, but takeoffs and landings frightened him.

In the co-pilot's seat was Nicky DeFranco, another one of Ricci's men. They called him "Bugs." Wallace had used him once before. DeFranco had bugged an opposing lawyer's office for Wallace prior to a critical arbitration meeting.

Ricci had mentioned using "a bug" in an earlier conversation, so Wallace called DeFranco and told him to meet him at the airport for a job. *Ricci must be really*

concerned or he wouldn't have wanted Stroh to be bugged.
He acknowledged DeFranco's presence with a wave after
selecting his seat.

"Hope you like the cockpit. I prefer a cabin seat," said
Wallace.

"It's more exciting up here," DeFranco responded.

"I guess it is. Are you here to help fly in addition to
doing the job?" asked Wallace.

"I'm always willing to learn new stuff," replied
DeFranco.

"Are you going to do the monitoring, too?" he asked.

"Nah, just setting it up…I'm going back tonight with
you… someone else will be coming tomorrow or the next
day."

"OK," replied Wallace nonchalantly.

DeFranco grunted an inaudible response as Whitney
started the engines. Wallace didn't respond. He gulped the
booze and relaxed a little.

The attorney had a fear of flying and would have
preferred another pilot other than the one Ricci called
"Zany." He didn't know if DeFranco could fly or not, but
the man seemed interested in Whitney's pre-flight
procedures.

As the plane lifted off the runway he felt a surge of
anxiety that lasted until the landing gear clunked into
place and the plane began to level off. He was almost able

to enjoy the patchwork pattern of farms, roads and lakes visible below.

Wallace sipped a second drink and began to ponder the meeting with Stroh. He had warned Stroh, in no uncertain terms, about the importance of accommodating Ricci. He hoped the senator had taken the warning seriously and also hoped his gut feeling – looming failure in this matter – was wrong and would go away. Stroh couldn't expect to simply return the money and forget the deal. There was more to it.

Wallace had worked for the Ricci family for nearly 20 years. He had been hired by Carmine Ricci and had become a trusted family adviser as well as chief legal counsel. He had managed to keep both father and son out of the reach of the law and the IRS through an elaborate array of, mostly legal, holding companies. His association with the Riccis had been lucrative but not one from which he could easily resign, shirk his responsibilities or be completely comfortable. Dominic Ricci was a dangerous and difficult man.

Still, he enjoyed the legal challenges of working for the Riccis and the complexities of their businesses. He had assured Ricci he was the only one that could handle the situation with Stroh: he understood the situation in the Legislature and he understood Stroh. Now he regretted the bold position he had taken and the confidence he had placed in the senator.

Wallace knew that Stroh coveted a U.S. congressional seat, and, although Ricci couldn't see to it that Stroh was elected, he certainly could see to it that he wasn't.

The casino proposal was controversial, but Wallace believed Stroh could still pass the legislation. After all, Stroh was a powerful and persuasive leader. Wallace admired his political skill. The senator needed to be reminded there would be great rewards for him when the legislation was signed into law.

And Stroh needed to be reminded, too, there would be serious problems for him if the legislation failed. Ricci might even threaten his life or worse.

Undoubtedly, the senator was unaccustomed to being challenged or intimidated by a man like Ricci. Wallace knew politicians were often the most susceptible to the mob's unique type of pressure and he hoped the meeting would go smoothly.

He settled in his seat and closed his eyes. He wanted to be rested and alert when he met with Stroh.

* * *

Stroh locked the hatch of the *Summer Breeze* and headed toward the parking lot where Anne waited in the car. As he walked, Stroh contemplated the appropriate way to convey his resolve to Wallace concerning the casino legislation and Ricci's money. His reflection was abruptly interrupted when he heard a familiar voice.

"Louis! Que pasa?"

It was Bob Wilkinson, shouting at him from the next pier. Wilkinson's cheerfulness annoyed Stroh.

"Bob, howareyuh?" Stroh shouted back.

"How about dinner tonight?"

"Thanks," said Stroh, "but we can't. Maybe on the weekend."

"Lemme know," shouted the other man. "Hello to Anne."

"Thanks," said Stroh as he hurried off.

Chapter 14

There was an air of sadness in the Ursula Shop throughout the day. Rosa was quite upset by Strawberry's death. Her close connection to the deceased and the policeman's visit had bothered Bartlett. He was thankful he hadn't been seen disposing of the body and thankful Strawberry had only shoved four pieces of mail into his pocket and nothing else. He should have checked the body more carefully before he hurriedly disposed of the corpse.

The message from Russo disturbed him. But he felt insulated because of Russo: the authorities could screw around with him for days and get nowhere. Russo was not committing a crime by relaying messages and it would be almost impossible to implicate him in any wrongdoing. They would have to catch me first, before they could involve Russo, he surmised. He hoped he was smart enough to never get caught.

Bartlett wondered if Russo was being careless. He had considered re-arranging his business before. Modern technology could eliminate the need for a Russo or the office in Chicago. With a computer, he could program a blind destination for business messages. In any case, he needed to contact Russo.

The Strawberry incident convinced him it might be a good time to leave St. Croix for a few days. He had been thinking about a short trip to Puerto Rico and about Denise Spangler, the real estate broker he'd met in St. Croix a few months earlier. He couldn't quite remember her face, but he vividly recalled her firm shape, stuffed into the tight red dress. She had encouraged him to call whenever he visited San Juan.

In the afternoon, Bartlett made a reservation on the evening flight to San Juan. He left a message for Rosa on her answering machine. He would be away for two nights but back in time for her to attend Strawberry's funeral. Before leaving, he checked to be sure she got the message.

Bartlett was glad to be going away for a short visit and hopeful the inept police investigators would quickly forget about solving the murder once the family buried the poor sonofabitch.

Chapter 15

Dr. Frederic Mancini's preference was to soak up sun and rum on the weekends. His job as island coroner wasn't as stressful as the wearied surgical practice he had abandoned years earlier. And the dead, for the most part, had been cooperative recently, dying from natural causes on weekdays. The young man who died in a moped accident near Cane's Bay interrupted his weekend plans.

The body was in the basement of the Richtner Funeral Home which also served as a morgue for the western side of the island. An autopsy was required and this appeared to be a fairly simple case: the young man had died by launching himself and his moped off a cliff.

Dr. Mancini was completing the autopsy report as Officer Caulier, lead investigator for the St. Croix police, ambled into the morgue.

"Anything unusual about this, doctor?"

Mancini disliked the way Caulier pronounced "doctor."

"Not really, it seems to be what it appears to be...his blood alcohol was nearly twice the limit and there were drugs in his system. The impact from the crash probably broke his neck and killed him. There's some unusual bruising on the neck and the trachea was crushed, which may not have resulted from the accident. But at this point I believe the death was probably accidental..."

Officer Caulier nodded. He didn't like Dr. Mancini or trust his diagnosis and he wondered if the death was accidental or not. He didn't have the evidence, budget or initiative to pursue a further investigation. St. Croix authorities rarely concerned themselves with cases involving the death of a criminal, particularly when drugs were involved.

"Maybe he had been stealing drugs," Mancini said. "There were enough of them in him."

"Maybe, it looks like he was stealing letters from mailboxes just before the accident...probably hoping for checks or credit cards. We have had some problems with him before."

"Well, everything's here on the report," said Mancini. "Just another drug-related dead man. I can look further into the bruising and trachea injury, if necessary..." He hoped it wouldn't be.

"No," said Caulier. "If you're finished with the report, I can take it now. Nothing more to do. We can turn the body over to the mortician. The family's ready to bury him."

Chapter 16

Stroh arrived at the Holland airport 20 minutes before Wallace was scheduled to land. It wasn't much more than a small asphalt runway on the outskirts of town, consisting of a few corrugated steel hangers, a parking lot and an office. Stroh remembered when it had been a farm.

Promptly at 8, the gleaming new Cessna touched down, taxied and stopped near the office. The pilot emerged, and, with almost military courtesy, lowered the stair for his passenger. It might have been a minor head of state arriving.

Stroh and Wallace were about the same age and there had been several intersections in their careers, but there hadn't been any direct involvement until the casino legislation materialized. Stroh regretted again accepting money from Ricci, but at the time he hadn't seen any alternative.

Wallace exited the plane. He was wearing a dark suit and a bright silk tie. Stroh thought he looked seriously overdressed for the warm summer evening. He thought of asking him "Where's the funeral?" but quickly changed his mind.

"Welcome to Holland." Stroh extended his hand for a firm, insincere handshake. "How was the flight?"

"Not bad," said Wallace. "I'm actually beginning to prefer the smaller planes. The drinks are better."

"My car's over here. I thought we'd go to a favorite place on Lake Macatawa for dinner. Are the pilots coming with us?"

"No, they stay with the plane. I'd like to be back here before 11."

"No problem," said Stroh. "We'll have a good dinner and get you back."

"I hope so," said Wallace quietly.

Preliminaries over, there was a long silence between the two men as Stroh drove toward the lake. Finally, Wallace asked, "Have you thought about our conversation?"

"Yes, of course...," said Stroh. "You know that getting this thing passed isn't a mechanical procedure. The political climate isn't what it was when we made our...arrangements. The governor's chosen this as an issue...he's even talking about changing the lottery...I don't think I need to tell you that I've done all I can."

"You might need to do more," said Wallace.

Stroh didn't believe that Wallace or Ricci could

threaten him with much more than mild embarrassment. Ricci wouldn't risk threatening the most powerful man in the Michigan Senate.

Another silence between the two men lasted for several minutes.

"Look," said Stroh, "I've decided to return Ricci's money." He pulled a small envelope from his pocket and placed it on the seat between them.

Wallace remained silent. He gave Stroh a blank stare, looked at the envelope and then shifted his attention back to the roadway.

"Tell Ricci I'll keep working on getting the bill passed and I won't expect anything in return."

Wallace listened carefully; there was a long pause before he responded.

"Stroh...the casino development is very, very important to Mr. Ricci. He made a strong commitment to you, and he's helped you in ways you probably aren't even aware of...he doesn't want the money back. He wants the casino bill. I understand how difficult this could be for you, but I want you to understand how important this is for me and Mr. Ricci."

His tone was ominous. Stroh sensed they weren't going to accomplish much. He felt an urge to turn the car around and deliver Wallace back to the airport. He wanted to be finished with Ricci and Wallace. He hadn't seen this side of Wallace's character before.

"We're almost there," said Stroh as he turned onto Lake Macatawa Drive. "I think you'll like this place."

"Good. I'm starved. Will Anne be joining us?"

"No, not this evening."

"Too bad, I wanted to meet her in person."

A warning light flashed momentarily in Stroh's mind.

*　　*　　*

A grotesque fiberglass pelican was perched on the roof of the Pelican Point Restaurant overlooking Lake Macatawa. Wallace and Stroh were seated by a window overlooking the lake.

After they ordered drinks and dinner another silence occupied the two men. Wallace finally spoke.

"Stroh, do you know where Ricci's family is from?"

"No," said Stroh, sensing that Wallace was about to deliver a prepared statement.

"The Riccis are from Calabria, a region in the southernmost part of Italy. Their family immigrated to Detroit from Locri, a small, agricultural village near the Mediterranean shore. Ricci's grandfather was a blacksmith there. He was also an important man in Locri. He helped people with their problems, helped them with money and helped them settle disputes. People listened to him and he was capable of doing many things for the people in the village.

"One day, the mayor of Locri, a headstrong man, refused to honor a simple request from Ricci's grandfather who had done many favors for the mayor. The mayor was asked again, and again he refused. Ricci's grandfather was very disappointed.

"Within days the mayor disappeared. He was never heard from again. Some said he ran away to America, but I don't think so.

"Ricci's grandfather was a compassionate man and he took care of the man's wife and children. He took very good care of the man's wife..."

Wallace paused.

"Yes?" said Stroh quizzically.

"That's all," said Wallace, "just a story about Ricci's grandfather. They're a fascinating family."

"Well, it's a curious story, but I'm not sure why you're telling me. Is it supposed to be a threat?"

"Of course not, you've seen too many movies, Stroh."

"Ricci's a businessman and you both should know better than to threaten me. We can have a long-term relationship that's good for all of us. But I can't do the impossible. Tell Ricci to be patient."

Stroh was feeling impatient and angry. He wanted to end the dinner and the conversation.

"Don't get upset senator. It was just a story," Wallace

said, sensing his mood.

They finished their meal in silence. After coffee was served, Wallace asked, "Did you know Anne's husband?"

"No," said Stroh, wondering why Wallace would ask. Anne had said very little about her ex-husband.

"He was a photographer," said Wallace. "Not a very good one, I am told, but I think his subject matter was excellent."

He reached into his jacket and pulled out an envelope which he handed to Stroh.

Stroh opened it and removed a group of photographs. They showed Anne naked, engaged in a variety of sexual actions with a man. Stroh felt like he'd been kicked in the solar plexus.

"Where'd you get these?" he sputtered.

Wallace didn't answer, but smiled slightly.

"Keep them," he said. "I've got others. She's quite a woman."

The drive to the airport was silent. Stroh felt sick and confused.

When they reached the airport, Wallace broke the silence.

"Think about our conversation, Louis. Let's get this business finished and behind us. Understand? But, don't take too long. Mr. Ricci's impatient. Thanks for dinner."

*   *   *

During the drive back to Saugatuck, Stroh felt alternately like sobbing and vomiting. His life had suddenly changed. The resolve he felt earlier in the day had turned into fear and revulsion. Wallace had threatened him and threatened Anne.

She was waiting for him when he entered the house. He couldn't look at her without seeing the photographs.

*   *   *

Whitney and DeFranco were standing near the hanger smoking a cigarette when Wallace returned.

"Did you get the house done?" Wallace asked DeFranco.

"Yeah, the girlfriend was very accommodating. She went for a long walk, and we were in and out in just a couple of minutes. We got bugs on the phones, in the bedroom and in the kitchen."

"Those wireless jobs are great," said Whitney. "The girlfriend's real nice too ... I like Stroh's taste."

"She's very attractive," said Wallace, "would you like to see more of her?"

"Whaddya mean?" said Whitney, interested.

"Never mind." said Wallace. "Are we ready to go?"

"Yup."

"Then, let's get out of here."

*   *   *

Wallace was up early the next morning. The meeting with Stroh had gone about as planned, except for the check. He was becoming increasingly anxious and doubtful about his influence on the senator. Stroh's initial enthusiasm and optimism for the casino legislation a year earlier was rapidly waning. Wallace had promised Ricci he could handle Stroh, but now he was unsure. He hoped the story and the photographs would convince Stroh that it would not be wise to cross Dominic Ricci. And, depending on the outcome of the casino legislation, Wallace wondered about his future with the Riccis too.

Just before noon, he phoned Ricci to report on the meeting. Wallace began, "He met me at 8 at the Holland airport. On our way to dinner, he tried to give me a $100,000 check. I didn't accept the money. I ignored the gesture. After we ate, I told him the story about your grandfather and showed him the pictures. I thought he was gonna bust when he saw the pictures. He was upset and I think he was afraid, but I'm not sure he can deliver...the Legislature's a strange place these days. I used DeFranco to bug the house. We got back around midnight."

Ricci was calm and controlled. "Keep in touch on this," he said. "We may need to push harder…maybe even take the broad…but let's wait and see. If we find out he is done with us and wants to make trouble, take care of it quickly. You know what to do."

In anticipation of problems, Ricci had previously given Wallace names and phone numbers of professionals who, for a price, would get rid of Sen. Louis Stroh or anyone else very quietly and quickly. Wallace had scribbled the information on a legal envelope which he had stuffed in his briefcase for safekeeping. He made a mental note to destroy the envelope if he ever had to use the information.

Stroh hadn't received a death sentence yet, but Ricci was becoming exceedingly impatient and worried. Stroh had tried to return the money, an action that was deemed uncooperative and naïve but not terrible. Nevertheless, Ricci wanted to know if Stroh was still worthy of their trust and still committed to the task. There was no reason to take a chance. And the bugs would make it easy to monitor the senator.

Wallace hoped Stroh would realize that his cooperation and assistance were absolutely essential to ensure his survival. Some progress, at this juncture, would be enough to temporarily appease Ricci. And he hoped Stroh absolutely understood it would be a fatal mistake to ignore Ricci's warnings.

Chapter 17

Bartlett retrieved Denise Spangler's business card from his office Rolodex. He called her office number.

"Denise Spangler," the voice answered seductively.

He instantly remembered her sexy voice. "Hi, it's Jim Bartlett. We met in St. Croix at the Salty Pirate Resort … in the bar, a couple of months ago..."

"I remember," she said. Her voice was warm and inviting. "You kept putting those tequila shots in front of me...I'll never forget you, or the headache I had. Are you in San Juan?"

"No, but I will be later today and I hoped we could meet and have dinner tonight. Are you free?"

She didn't hesitate. "Sure," she said, "but no tequila...I have to work tomorrow."

"I promise," he said.

"I'll bet you do," she said, laughing gently.

"I have a reservation at the Conquistador Hotel, near

the airport. Would you like to meet there, have a drink, and then decide on dinner?"

"That's fine," she said, "When?"

"My flight arrives at 7. Can we meet in the cocktail lounge at 8 and then take it from there?"

"OK," she said.

"If I'm going to be later, I'll call. I'm looking forward to seeing you again."

"Good," she said. "It'll be nice to see you again, too. See you at 8."

"I can hardly wait," he said.

The rest of the day, Bartlett eagerly anticipated the evening trip to San Juan. Upon returning from work, he quickly packed and added extra condoms to his kit. He hoped the late afternoon downpour wouldn't delay his flight.

Strawberry's death and Officer Caulier's visit were troubling. And he hoped there weren't too many complications awaiting him in Chicago with Russo. *It will be good to get away.*

The rain slowed as he made the short drive to the St. Croix International airport. The squeaking brakes on the Jeep, reminded him it was time to get them repaired.

The customs officer gave him a nod as he passed through the security gate. The recognition made him feel uncomfortable, but he was a regular customer and St.

Croix was a small island. He wondered who else might be recognizing him there.

He took an aisle seat on the plane and admired the dark complected, long-legged stewardess as he settled in for the short flight. He noticed her perfectly-shaped buttocks as she moved the drink cart down the aisle. Her perfume smelled alluringly delicious. He was anxious to see Denise.

He tried to nap during the 30-minute flight, but he was edgy and nervous. The investigation of Strawberry's death was a nagging thought.

San Juan International Airport seemed huge and busy after the funky terminal in St. Croix. Bartlett needed a few minutes to adjust to the brisk pace.

He took a shuttle bus to the Conquistador where he registered and paid for his room. The suite was freshly decorated and comfortable and there was a splendid view of the beach. He hoped Denise would enjoy it. His anticipation increased. He hurriedly showered and quickly dressed for dinner.

Before heading to the bar, Bartlett sat on the bed and dialed the number Russo had left.

Russo answered.

"This is JBS."

"Russo, where the hell are you?"

"At my girlfriend's, don't worry. It's secure here. A guy from Detroit came into the office and it kinda freaked me out...I thought you'd wanna know about it right away."

"What guy from Detroit?"

"Henry Wallace. Said he's an attorney."

"What did he want?"

"Said he wanted to get in touch with you, said he wanted me to arrange it."

"How did he know where the office was?"

"I dunno. He just showed up."

"Give me his number."

"Hold on, I got it here..."

Bartlett wrote the number down. The lawyer's unexpected appearance at the office shocked him.

"Listen carefully. I want you to close up the office immediately and find another one."

"It's all paid for through the month..."

"Don't worry about it. Get your stuff out of there and find another office. Also, change the office name to FDR Services."

"Hey that's my initials...cool."

"Listen to me Russo. Don't transfer the phone number to the new place, like before. I'll see to that."

"It's gonna cost a little bit...I just changed the place a while ago."

"Just do it. This is what I pay you to do," Bartlett said,

obviously annoyed with Russo's hesitation.

"Are you unhappy with this job?"

"No, why?"

"Then do it exactly as I'm telling you. Do you understand?

"Yes sir."

"Call my answering service when you've got a new setup going."

Bartlett slammed the phone down on the receiver before Russo could respond. *Maybe it's time to rethink my arrangements. I probably should return to Chicago and get rid of Russo. He has become a liability.*

Chapter 18

Sunlight was streaming into the bedroom when Anne awoke. It was 10:30 and already another hot day. Louis was still asleep. He had been anxious and upset when he returned from his meeting with Wallace. He had consumed too many scotches. He had made love to her in a rough, almost violent way that she had never experienced with him before. Unhappily, it had reminded her of her ex-husband.

Her movement awakened Stroh. He suddenly looked tired and old to Anne.

"How did you sleep?" she asked.

"OK."

She could tell he was hung over.

"What happened at the meeting?" she asked.

Stroh stared at her for a moment. She thought she saw tears forming in his eyes.

He pulled her to him. "I love you very much," he said,

with his familiar tenderness. "I'll tell you about the meeting later..."

Anne knew when to end her questions.

"Would you like some coffee?"

"Yes," he said.

"I'll bring it to you."

Stroh's headache made thinking difficult. But he knew he wasn't going to end his career or his relationship with Anne because of Ricci or Wallace or the casino gambling bill or the goddamn photographs.

I have more resources than they imagine. They are foolish to threaten me. I have many friends in business, politics, law enforcement and the judicial that I could call upon for help. A big-time lawyer and a mob boss could be vulnerable, too.

Chapter 19

In the dimly lit Tropical Bar, at the Conquistador, the piano player had just begun playing *Morning of the Carnival* when Bartlett strolled in. He swayed a little with the music. He saw Denise seated at the bar. She looked wonderful; sophisticated, exotic and sexy.

"You are more beautiful than I remembered," he whispered in her ear when he approached. Smiling, she turned to greet him. As they kissed his hand brushed her breasts.

"And you are more handsome than I remember!" she said, laughing. Her dark eyes and her laughter were captivating. She was beautiful, and he realized how hungry he was for her body.

"Would you like a drink?" he asked.

"I already have a vodka martini. You should try one, they are quite good."

"Yes, I'll have one, too."

Denise signaled the bartender and another cocktail quickly appeared.

"I've missed you," Bartlett said.

"But you hardly know me, how could you miss me?" she replied, with laughter in her voice.

"I know you well enough to miss you."

"That's a good answer," she said. "I'll accept it!"

Bartlett's appreciation of Denise, her laughing eyes and quick smile increased as he sipped his martini. He hadn't felt such warmth in quite a while; he wanted to embrace her then and there. She seemed to understand.

"What's your room number?" she asked. "I'll have Roberto send up a pitcher of martinis...we can watch the sunset before dinner."

"The sun set a half hour ago," said Bartlett.

"I know," she said.

Denise performed a slow and elegant striptease in the softly-lit hotel room. She wanted to please Bartlett and she was succeeding admirably. He was grateful for the presence of this sensual, full-bodied woman.

Slowly and tenderly, Bartlett kissed her lips, her face, her neck and her breasts. The affection he felt was powerful; he wanted to reciprocate the pleasure she gave him. Denise remembered the skillful lover she had met in St. Croix, and she was fully responsive to his touch. She gave herself to him completely.

With the exception of Moira, Bartlett had desired only sexual relationships with women. But tonight he felt a strange surge of emotion and tenderness. He understood that his life was beginning to change.

When he awoke Wednesday morning, Denise was still asleep. She had spent the last two nights in bed with him. He admired her naked form. He gently kissed her cheek and smoothed her hair with his hand. He wanted more time to be with her, but there wasn't any more time. He had arranged for an early morning flight back to St. Croix. He hurriedly showered, packed and quietly left the room after enjoying one final look at Denise in the plush, king-size bed.

Chapter 20

The commercial jet from San Juan landed five minutes early at St. Croix International. Bartlett located his Jeep and drove directly to the Ursula Shop. Rosa was sorting mail when he briskly entered the store. Her greeting was warm and pleasant; he was glad her mood had improved.

They chatted briefly about inventory shortages, customer requests and a stateside trip that he had unexpectedly decided upon. "I will be leaving tomorrow for at least a week," Bartlett said.

She wanted to ask about the need for another trip so soon since the last, but she avoided the urge. "I'll take care of everything while you're away," Rosa said. "Don't forget I will be attending the two o'clock funeral service today...I doubt if I get back to close." Her tone was matter-of-fact.

"Don't worry about it...please convey my sincere condolences to your friend."

"Thanks…I will tell her how sorry you are about her brother."

"That's fine," he said. "I'm on the early morning flight tomorrow…I'll stay in touch."

Just then, a tourist entered the store and interrupted their conversation. Rosa excused herself and went to the counter to help.

Bartlett headed for his office. The incident with Strawberry seemed far away. Alone at his desk, Bartlett thought about the pleasureful two evenings with Denise and the need to fly back to Chicago.

He wondered, who Wallace was, who he worked for and how he had found the JBS office? Wallace's request for a personal meeting was dangerous and unacceptable.

*   *   *

Early Thursday morning, a sandy haze filled the air as Bartlett boarded the flight, first to Miami and then connecting to O'Hare International. He could feel the grit on his face, and it reminded him of his arrival at Tan Son Nhut Air Force base.

Closing his eyes, he remembered the sensations when he exited the commercial plane that had carried him from Chicago to Seattle to Saigon. He descended the jet's stairway into an atmosphere of stifling humidity, dust and grit like a heavy fog that hung in the air. It had seemed strange, dangerous and exciting; he had felt a peculiar combination of fear and exhilaration. Thirty-six hours earlier he had been in his Chicago home. Now, he was in a war zone more than a world away.

He had gone to Vietnam with the 9th Infantry from Fort Riley, Kan., for his tour of duty in early 1967. Dong Tam, the base camp where he was assigned, had been built on top of a rice paddy southwest of Saigon. It was located in the muddy Mekong Delta region.

When he had arrived, the division was fully involved in search and destroy missions against the Vietcong. The VC were a disciplined and elusive enemy, supported by the regimes in North Vietnam and China.

The terrain -- marshes, rice paddies and swamps -- were treacherous and he learned quickly that the small, delicate Vietnamese people could also be treacherous. Women, children and white-haired grandmothers carried rifles and grenades. It wasn't the kind of battle his brief combat training had prepared him for.

He remembered his first firefight, his fear and the dreamlike qualities of the experience. All of his senses were heightened. The incoming projectile seemed like an image from a cartoon, and he could hear the trailing whistle. It sounded like the Fourth of July. The rocket exploded 30 feet in front of him, in the spot where Michael Killian had been standing the moment before. Mud, blood and flesh were splattered everywhere on the ground. Bartlett wasn't sure if he was hit or not. He could sense nothing, only his fear.

Bartlett remembered standing and firing his M16 in the direction of the enemy. Later, he had decided his actions were purely unconscious. But the sound of the rifle firing made him feel vengeful and powerful; he might have screamed. He couldn't remember.

He wanted to kill; he knew it. He wanted to annihilate the enemy who had attacked him and obliterated Michael Killian. Bartlett felt a cold, focused grim purpose: he suddenly knew what war was about.

The firing stopped as suddenly as it had started and he advanced slowly, parting the tall marsh grass. He could hear the enemy retreating, and he fired in the direction of the sounds. He heard a painful cry and knew he had hit an unseen target.

He moved cautiously until he came upon a Vietnamese man, clothed in what looked like black pajamas, writhing in the mud and grass. His leg was shattered by a bullet and he was bleeding profusely. His AK-47 lay in the mud at his side. His feet looked absurdly small and delicate.

The sergeant appeared from behind and looked at the man, obviously in pain, and then looked at Bartlett. "Get rid of him," he said, "unless you want to carry him back to camp."

Bartlett looked into the dark eyes and boyish face of the fallen man and then, without hesitating, shot him in the head. He kicked the corpse and it was lifelike for a moment, and then it settled in the mud. The sights and smells of death were everywhere: torn flesh, blood, urine, perspiration and shit. He knew then he would never forget it.

He returned to what had been Michael Killian. The sergeant was retrieving his tags. Bartlett didn't know whether to feel sorry for Killian or for the soldiers who had survived the battle; he knew his life had been changed forever. Killian had been there only a few weeks.

Another soldier slogged by and, patting Bartlett on the back, said "Forget it boy, it ain't nothin'." The words were nonsensical, but the attempt to comfort eased the pain. Killian's death seemed random and pointless, and it seemed more like a disappearance than a death.

Killian had become a friend. Bartlett thought about those for whom Killian's life had meaning: parents, two brothers, a girlfriend and unknown others. This was their tragedy now; Killian had no choice.

Bartlett thought about Killian and the others who he had seen perish, and concluded there was purpose to a soldier's death there. This was not about politics, it was about mortal combat and men trained to kill each other. There was no debate about right or wrong on the battlefield. Killian lived and died honorably, in a kill or be killed environment.

*   *   *

The pleasant but insincere voice of a nearby stewardess brought Bartlett back to the present. He ordered a double scotch on the rocks.

He tilted his seat back and sipped his drink. The casualties of war were many: Killian and thousands like him, thousands of Vietcong, thousands of innocents. The totals were unimaginable. And perhaps Bartlett himself. He had seen terrible suffering: fathers and mothers carrying their screaming children away from the battlefield, the wounded clinging to life and grasping for it. Screams. Cries for help. The horrors of death delivered by soldiers in combat. A horrible war in a beautiful place. A war of contrasts in a land of contrasts, where nothing was quite what it seemed to be. That war was over, but Bartlett's war continued. He sighed, finished his drink and closed his eyes again.

Chapter 21

Bartlett was perspiring and almost nauseous when he opened his eyes again. Sometimes the combination of alcohol and air travel made him sick. Or was it the dream that had been unusually vivid, with the recurring images of Vietnam? No matter, he was awake now. *It was a miracle I survived the snakes, booby traps, bullets, mortars and bombs.*

The clatter of cans and bottles on the refreshment cart awakened him fully. Flight attendants were preparing the cabin for landing. He checked his watch; right on time. The Miami skyline was visible through the window. Life there seemed miniaturized and distant.

When the plane touched down and arrived at the gate, the passengers rapidly began to pop open the overhead compartments, awaiting their anxious surge toward the exit. Bartlett wondered why they hurried and what awaited them in Miami: vacation, aging parents, husbands or wives. He felt heaviness about his purposes, almost a premonition.

Stiff and tired, he rose and stretched and reminded himself to fly first-class on his next long-distance trip. He gathered his coat and shoulder bag from the overhead compartment and deplaned.

In his coat pocket he could feel the envelope he had retrieved from his mother's jewelry box after her death. He often carried it to remind himself of her.

He remembered when he returned from Vietnam to bury her. He was numb to death, even hers. The Army chaplain, quietly and compassionately, had given him the bad news. It wasn't until he reached her tiny apartment that he felt a sob emerge. Her life and death had been lonely ... but she had peace now.

There had been an eerie quiet in the tiny apartment when he arrived to make her final arrangements. He sorted through her modest belongings without emotion until he came to her jewelry box. When he looked inside, he felt like he had arrived at the hidden center of her universe. There was a funereal quality to the arrangement of items inside: his father's watch, some ancient costume jewelry, a small packet of financial papers and, in a worn manila envelope, a letter Bartlett had written her from Vietnam. It was obvious she had read it many times.

He remembered well the circumstances when the letter was written: Dong Tam, August 9, 1967, just prior to going on patrol. At the time he thought it might be his last letter. From all the letters he had written to her, he wondered why she had saved this one.

Inside the terminal, Bartlett stopped for a coffee at a crowded chain restaurant. He took the envelope from his pocket and carefully removed the letter and a neatly-folded red silk scarf.

Before he left for the war, his mother had given him the scarf. "For memory and good luck," she had told him. He had hidden it in his kit and carried it through the war. Perhaps it was lucky. He imagined the scarf still had a hint of his mother's scent. After her death, he had placed the scarf in the envelope with the letter. They belonged together.

Now he unfolded the letter and read it again, remembering the very young man who had written it:

Mom, Got your letter. It was good to hear about our old neighborhood and I'm glad you're doing well. It reminds me that there are still places where people aren't trying to kill each other.

We're getting ready to go on patrol. There's been a lot of fighting and the base camp gets mortar fire almost every night. Our platoon got into a firefight yesterday but we only lost one man. We got 10 of them, maybe more.

I'm getting used to conditions here. Camp is OK if you can get used to the heat, bugs and latrines, but I have trouble sleeping. Everyone does. A few of the new ones cry like babies at night.

Don't worry about me. I'm taking good care of myself. I still have your lucky scarf.

Hope you and Stan are getting along. Stay away from him when he's drinking. He's OK when he's not.

Not much time now. Will write more later. Love, John.

He refolded the letter and scarf and put them back in the envelope. So much had changed since he had written that letter. And so much was unchanged. He was still on patrol in a war zone.

Chapter 22

Bartlett's flight landed at O'Hare International just after 5. The heat, humidity and exhaust fumes outside the terminal almost sickened Bartlett. He had forgotten how unpleasant Chicago could be on a hot summer day.

He hailed the first cab in the line, an old battered Chevy. "Blake Hotel on Michigan," he told the driver as he swung his bags into the back seat.

"Longer ride tonight," said the driver. "Lot of traffic on the expressway this time." He spoke with a sing-song Middle Eastern accent.

"I've got plenty of time," said Bartlett in an insincere attempt to be cordial.

The scenery along the expressways hadn't changed and the pavement still needed repair. The adjacent buildings and retaining walls on the expressway were covered in patches with graffiti. The shoulders were littered with broken glass, shreds of tires and various car parts. And there was an occasional lost shoe, a sight which always puzzled Bartlett.

Traffic was heavy. The cab, which smelled of stale smoke and stale food, drifted from one lane to another, bouncing like a carnival ride. Bartlett could see the nicotine stains on the driver's fingers. Mohammed Seatar was the name on the license attached to the visor; the picture showed a man with a narrow, wizened, sun-dried face.

Several minor accidents on the expressway made the normal 30-minute drive to the Loop longer. Bartlett was relieved when the silhouette of the Blake Hotel appeared on the skyline. The elegant old hotel was his favorite place to stay in Chicago. He especially liked the restaurant, found on the hotel's street level. Their menu featured fish and beef; he always ordered Dover sole there.

He tipped the cabbie and noticed again the yellow tint of his fingertips. The cabbie nodded a solemn thank you. The doorman at the hotel greeted Bartlett in almost familiar fashion, something that always made him feel uncomfortable.

The cool atmosphere of the Blake was a welcome change from the heat and odors of the city outside. Bartlett was impressed anew by the marble floors and columns and the stately elegance of the building. He made a note to treat himself to a good scotch in the intimate little bar, near the front entrance.

He had made his reservation in the name of "Paul Stewart" and handed the prissy, sandy-haired desk clerk a credit card and an Illinois driver's license, which he used on his stateside trips. "My reservation is until next Friday, but I might need to stay longer," Bartlett said.

"We certainly will be pleased to accommodate your needs, Mr. Stewart. However, we would require a 24-hour notice to change your reservation. Here's your key. You're in 1502, overlooking the lake. Would you like a bellman, sir?"

"Yes," said Bartlett. "Have him put my bags in the room. I'll be up a bit later."

He handed the clerk a $20 bill and said, "Split this with him."

The clerk thanked him, and Bartlett turned and headed toward the stairway leading to the bar.

The narrow, dimly-lit bar was decorated like an expensive gentleman's club. Bartlett selected a plush upholstered booth in one corner, seeking a commanding view of his surroundings, a habit developed in the bars and strip joints in Vietnam.

He ordered a J & B on the rocks from an attractive but tired-looking waitress. Bartlett was aware the soft lighting flattered her.

When she returned with his drink she complimented him on his tan. Bartlett was amused by her flirtatiousness. She probably saw a parade of prosperous middle-aged businessmen. She would be surprised if she knew his profession.

The little bar was filled with people, and Bartlett carefully watched as more patrons filed in the doors. He was a faithful student of human behavior, and was always observant, always on guard, always looking for something out of place.

The scotch soothed and relaxed him. He welcomed the feeling. He'd lived his life on constant alert, and for too long. He was ready for a change.

He was glad to be back in Chicago and at the Blake. He was miles and lifetimes away from the neighborhood where he'd grown up. The small booth with the corner window seat reminded Bartlett of the rickety kitchen booth where he'd religiously done his homework as a child. His teachers always praised him for being an extremely bright student. No wonder, with few friends and him being somewhat withdrawn, he had more than enough time to study.

Bartlett always regretted his inability to attend college due to lack of funds. He qualified for student loans but he decided not to take advantage of the help. At the time, with the Vietnam War raging on, the service seemed like his only viable option. He signed on for a three-year enlistment in the Army.

As he slowly sipped his drink, Bartlett assessed his plans for the following day. In the morning, he would go to the downtown public library and look for information on Wallace. He wanted his business address, home address, phone numbers and, possibly, an abridged personal resume, too.

Bartlett wanted to contact Russo next and maybe drive by Russo's girlfriend's house in the afternoon. He was tempted to visit Moira.

When the waitress offered another drink, he accepted. She was suddenly more attractive to him.

With the third scotch, Bartlett was entirely relaxed. It had been a long day; two flights and the wild cab ride from O'Hare. He looked forward to a hot shower, a change of clothes, and a good meal and, if lucky, a willing partner for sex.

When the waitress arrived with the tab, Bartlett paid for his drinks and handed her a $20 bill.

"I appreciate good service," he said with a smile.

"Well thank you," she purred. She was friendly and flirtatious. Bartlett was encouraged.

"My name's Paul Stewart," he said. "I'm staying here at the hotel. I have a dinner reservation for two in the Seafood Grill at 10 ...would you like to join me?"

She paused. She certainly wasn't offended by the offer. "I'm Cheryl. I'm flattered that you'd ask, but I'm working till two and anyhow my boyfriend probably wouldn't approve. But, thanks for asking, Paul."

"I'm disappointed," said Bartlett. "You're very attractive and I'd like to learn more about you"

"You're sweet," she said, giving him a gentle squeeze on the arm as she slowly placed the $20 in her change purse and picked up his empty glass. Bartlett was impressed by her warmth and the clever, insincere response. She probably got dozens of invitations.

Bartlett returned to his room and took a long, soothing shower. He lay on the bed, closed his eyes and imagined what the evening would have been like if he had been with Cheryl. He had hoped for a passionate, anonymous encounter. But the enticingly friendly waitress would have only been a diversion for him now.

Before meeting Moira, he had been comfortable with his solitary life that featured only an occasional woman for his own well-being. He had relied on no one and trusted no one to share his life. But to his surprise, Moira had quickly become important to him and he had begun to open to her. Now, as he drifted into sleep, he wished she were there lying beside him.

Chapter 23

The next morning, Bartlett took a cab to the Chicago Public Library. He easily found Henry Wallace listed in a Michigan state law registry. The current Detroit phone book indicated Wallace resided in Birmingham, a Detroit suburb, and his address and phone number was included. A "Who's Who" directory provided a brief summary of Wallace, including highlights of his long-standing career. Bartlett copied all the items for future reference.

The Chicago phone book was missing from the shelf under the phone in his hotel room. He obtained a copy at the library and, to his dismay, found JBS Personnel Service listed in the directory.

The street address for JBS was in the white pages. *No wonder Wallace had been able to walk right into the office.* He had wondered if Wallace might have used a cross reference service to match JBS to the phone number.

Russo hadn't used the name of JBS in the answering machine message, because he had checked. Apparently Russo had forgotten his implicit instructions to make sure the number was unlisted. *Such a simple but dangerous mistake.* Bartlett was angry with himself for allowing Russo to screw things up. Russo's usefulness to him was about over.

When Bartlett went to leave, an unexpected downpour kept him in the library because he had forgotten his coat. He used the time to research the current and past business directories for U.S. and U.S territories. He noted his shop was not listed. Also, he was relieved to find no mention of "John Bartkowski" in any of the old Chicago city directories.

The only trace of John Bartkowski's existence would be found in medical, school, court and service records. Years ago, he had legally changed his name from John Bartkowski to John Moore, taking his mother's maiden name. But he had abandoned that name almost immediately after the paperwork was signed.

He was sure Coles had thoroughly researched John Bartkowski's records after the Brezinski assassination. Coles knew about John Moore, too. Bartlett wasn't worried; there was no connection to him through John Bartkowski, John Moore or Emery Clements. Moore had vanished even more quickly than Emery Clements had vanished from New Orleans.

Paul Stewart was one of several identities Bartlett often used when traveling on assignment. And there was no connection to Bartkowski through Stewart, either.

After the rain, the air was thick and humid. Bartlett noted the pavement was almost dry. The hurried Michigan Avenue crowds reminded him that he was accustomed to the slower rhythms of Christiansted.

Hungry, Bartlett walked into a funky, old-fashioned diner near the Tribune Building for lunch. It was noisy, greasy and crowded. Soon there wouldn't be many places like this, located right off Michigan Avenue, left to enjoy. The city he knew as a boy had almost entirely disappeared; he had almost entirely disappeared.

He ordered a cheeseburger and a Coke. The meal reminded him of when he, his younger brother, Steve, and his father would go to a Cubs baseball game. They always ate outside the ballpark because the sandwiches and drinks there were less expensive than at Wrigley Field. *Those were good times.*

Casually eating his sandwich and sipping his drink, he planned the rest of his day. First, he wanted to call Wallace and perhaps then Russo. Moira would have to wait for another time. He was probably going to be on assignment and he didn't want further complications.

* * *

Henry Wallace was alone in his office when the phone rang. He assumed it was Ricci and he paused before he answered.

"Henry Wallace?"

"Yes."

"JBS Personnel Service told me to contact you."

Wallace hesitated a moment, caught his breath and then spoke. "Thanks for calling. I've got a business client with a personnel problem and I was told you could help. I've been told you are reliable and efficient."

"Yes ... what do you have in mind?"

"We're thinking of terminating an employee but we want to evaluate the situation first. Could we meet and talk?" Wallace's words were rapid and nervous.

"We can talk now."

"I suppose we can...I should ask you what your fees are..."

"Twenty-five. Fifteen up front."

"Twenty-five! We might not need the full range of services..."

"That's why the fifteen up front. It could be a lot less, depending on what I do. I'll work with you."

"Well, we'd like to retain you to...look over the situation for now. Shall I send you a check?"

"No checks. I'm going to give you the name of a bank and an account number. As soon as the retainer is wired to the account, I'll contact you again."

"Well, let me give you some background..."

"I'll contact you after the money arrives," Bartlett stated, after giving Wallace the necessary banking information. The attorney was just about to ask another question, when he heard the phone click signaling the man had ended the call.

Wallace was nervous and sweating. He had never hired a hit man and he had never, before now, been involved in any serious criminal activity. Originally, he had been hired by the Riccis as an advisor for their legitimate business operations. He was a lawyer, not a criminal. But for now, Louis Stroh was his personal responsibility. He recalled Ricci's instructions: "I am depending on you to see this thing through, Wallace. You take care of it." Ultimately, he knew what those instructions meant.

Wallace wondered if Ricci would object to the manner in which he was proceeding. After all, he was hiring a hit man even though it might not be necessary to kill Louis Stroh. Wallace had built a solid reputation on always being well prepared. In case of a problem, he wanted to be ready.

Wallace decided to personally pay for the up-front deposit. He wasn't sure Ricci would reimburse him for the expense or not. Nevertheless, if Stroh got out of control and talked to the authorities, Ricci would hold him personally responsible. He knew what Ricci was capable of doing. Several minutes later, he hurriedly called his banker and arranged to transfer the funds.

Chapter 24

She needed time to think about herself. Moira Gray repeated this to herself many times during the drive from Evanston to South Haven. She hadn't taken a vacation in more than a year and she realized she was protecting herself from loneliness by losing herself in her job. Her assistant seemed relieved when Moira announced her plans.

She enjoyed the small towns and resorts along the southeastern shore of Lake Michigan. South Haven, Saugatuck and Holland had interesting little shops, bed & breakfast places to stay and plenty of casual dining restaurants. The Michigan shore was a welcome change from the business and bigness of Chicago.

The small farms in rural Michigan were a pleasant reminder of her childhood in Iowa. She had traveled alone to South Haven and Saugatuck several times after she first arrived in Chicago, and had spent a memorable week with Bartlett there, too.

In South Haven, Moira stopped for lunch at Alexandra's, a well-known eatery. It was after 2 and the crowd had thinned. The waiter, a tall, tanned, dark-haired young man seated her at a window booth. He was nervous and athletic. She watched him quickly appraise her body and she was flattered by his flirtatious attentiveness. She was still noticed.

An affectionate couple lingering over drinks in another booth reminded her of dining here with Bartlett. He had touched and nuzzled and kissed her, like the couple she was watching. She'd realized then she didn't want to lose his affection. His sudden and mysterious departure was still an unhealed wound for her. *It had been more than a year and a half since he had gone away and almost two years since they had been at Alexandra's.*

She felt more like a widow than an abandoned lover. Bartlett's disappearance was sudden and final, like a death. Like her father's death, when she was 15. *The great disappearing act.* She felt she knew Bartlett would return if he could. But she understood she couldn't spend her life waiting for him. *She needed time to think about herself.*

The waiter reappeared with coffee and a salad. Moira gave him an encouraging smile and watched the blood rush to his face. He was very young.

As Moira sipped her coffee, she thought about her vacation. She had booked a pool-side room at the Riverside Hotel in Saugatuck and would spend a lazy week there.

She would work on a tan, do some reading, and, perhaps, meet someone interesting. The night spots in Saugatuck were full of prosperous, horny, middle-aged men, she imagined. And one of them might be the beneficiary of her decision to have some selfish fun. *Bartlett would understand. He should understand how much she missed him.*

Moira remembered the day Bartlett moved some of his personal things into her Evanston home. His downtown apartment was as neat, clean and impersonal as an unoccupied hotel room. The furniture and belongings that remained made the rooms seem no emptier than they had been before. A month after his departure, she went to check for him at the apartment and discovered it had been vacated weeks earlier. The landlord didn't know anything about the disposition of the contents.

The empty rooms reminded Moira of Bartlett's peculiar ability to disappear emotionally. At times when they had been together, she knew that he wasn't present at all. She teased him about it, and one time she had asked if he were The Invisible Man. At first she worried that he was concealing a wife or another relationship, but intuitively she dismissed that thought. There was something in his life separate, distinct and troubling. Whatever it was, she wanted to help him with it. Twice, after he left, she had dreamt she had given birth to their child and the infant was a miniature Bartlett.

Still, her affection for him was strong and obvious despite his distant moments. She felt connected to him as she had been to no other man. He knew her moods and emotions and respected them. She laughed at herself; after her divorce, the therapist had asked her to carefully consider the kinds of men she chose. *Complicated. I choose complicated men.* She knew that Bartlett, wherever he was, still felt connected to her. *She would know if he didn't.*

She finished her lunch and left the restaurant after giving the young waiter a flirtatious look he wouldn't quickly forget.

On the road to Saugatuck, she noticed a shabby farmhouse next to a decrepit barn. It was another reminder of her childhood home. She remembered the scents of damp hay, milk and manure. She hadn't realized how poor they were until she moved to Chicago. She also realized what little difference it made. She had learned on the farm to trust her feelings and intuition, and she had also learned to accept life as it arrived.

She smiled as she drove. *I choose complicated men.*

Chapter 25

The night desk clerk seemed perturbed when Bartlett informed him late Saturday night of his change of plans. "I will be departing on Sunday," he said. "I know I'm not giving a 24-hour notice, but my business requires me to leave. Will there be a penalty?"

"Not this time," said the clerk. "I will waive the additional day charge ... but, next time; try to give us better notice."

"Thanks, I will."

Sunday morning Bartlett awoke, ate breakfast and began packing to leave. His preparations for an assignment were careful and thorough. He added two untraceable guns -- a 9 mm and a .25 caliber -- to his kit which included tools, duct tape, timers and plastic explosives. Hurriedly Saturday night he had been shopping on the south side of Chicago for guns and explosives. They were always available if you knew where to go.

He felt a kind of grim enthusiasm about the assignment, the same sort of feeling he remembered before going on patrol in Vietnam. There was also a sense of relief. He had decided to make this assignment his last.

Strangely, he had a sense of Moira's presence, as if she were near or about to enter the room. He wanted more than anything to be with her now. *After this ... he told himself.*

He carefully packed the kit inside his suitcase. He wiped his prints from the water glass, door handles and telephone and carefully rechecked the room. When he left, he knew he was on the verge of abandoning his old life forever.

He was ready to contact Wallace about the assignment. The bank representative had confirmed a $15,000 deposit, credited to his Cayman account. He was pleased Wallace had acted so promptly.

The last assignment. The thought brought a smile to his face. He was aware of the danger. He couldn't afford to be careless.

On the street level of the Blake Hotel, there was an old-fashioned mahogany telephone booth located near the elevators. Bartlett opened the glass door, entered and telephoned Wallace.

The number rang twice before Bartlett heard the firm and calculating voice say, "Henry Wallace."

"This is JBS. We received your retainer. Thank you."

There was a short pause and then Wallace responded. "Good, I have the information you'll need. The subject is Louis Stroh. He's vacationing in Saugatuck, Mich., at 315 Lake View Drive. You won't have any trouble finding his place. We just need you to watch him, for now...but if I need more, is there another way I can contact you? I want you prepared to move quickly...any questions? Oh, by the way, Stroh is the Michigan Senate majority leader."

"How often do you want updates?"

"Daily would be fine...mornings would be best," said Wallace.

"It's really not my business, but this deal is not my thing. Why don't you hire a private investigator? I appreciate the money, but ..."

"P.I.'s don't offer the kinds of services you provide."

"Enough said, I understand. I'll call daily around ten," said Bartlett.

"One more thing ...," said Wallace. "We'd like you to include his girlfriend, Anne Bishop, in the evaluation ..."

"That wasn't part of our deal. If you need an additional evaluation, there would be an extra charge. We'll talk about it tomorrow morning, let me think about it."

As soon as Bartlett hung up the phone, Wallace took a deep breath and gazed out his window and sat motionless in his chair. The line between legitimacy and criminality had been crossed. There was no turning back. He'd done some unpleasant and unethical things for Ricci before, but nothing like this. He was conspiring to possibly commit murder. And the guy from JBS, the killer, knew who he was and what he had done. He might need to discuss the consultant's future with Ricci later. He wondered how Ricci would handle the situation.

After several minutes of deliberation, Wallace picked up the phone and called Stroh. He wanted to make certain that Stroh understood how strongly Ricci felt about the casino legislation. And he wanted to do everything humanly possible to avoid having to order Stroh and his girlfriend's deaths.

Stroh's answering machine picked up the call. Wallace left a message; "I just wanted to remind you again, senator, of how important we feel this casino legislation is ... please call me immediately when you have something to report."

Wallace felt he'd made the situation, and its dangers, very clear to Stroh. Now he was fully prepared to wait and monitor Stroh and the casino legislation and, thanks to DeFranco, much more easily.

*   *   *

The hustle of people and endless traffic on Stoney Island Avenue was natural to characters like Willie Jackson. He had grown up early in the rough, mostly black, 38th street, South Chicago district. The neighborhood had spawned a wide variety of criminals; drug dealers, prostitutes, con men and thieves.

His mother worked days as a maid and she spent nights trying to care for her eight children. It was a hard life, but young Jackson had managed to survive. He had been busted twice before his 16th birthday for serious infractions, but he had avoided incarceration by selling information to the cops. Being a snitch was a danger, but there were rewards. The cops paid fairly well and his criminal career was mostly ignored.

One of his contacts in the Chicago PD was Detective David Coles. Occasionally, Coles would ask around for information about a particular crime. Jackson had been helpful in the past. Following the Brezinski murder, Coles had asked around about a tanned, dark-haired, middle-aged white man who may have bought a 9 mm handgun in the neighborhood. There had been a few leads, but Bartkowski hadn't materialized.

*   *   *

Early Sunday morning, Coles was on his second stale cup of coffee, trying to wake up, when he was startled by the intercom. First a buzz, and then the annoying crackling voice of the homely receptionist, stating, "Detective Coles ... I got a man on the phone for you. He won't give his name. Says he needs to talk to you."

"OK, put him on." Seconds later he heard the familiar click of a transferred call. "Detective Coles," he said.

"Coles?"

"Yeah. Who's this?"

"It's Willie Jackson. Maybe I got somethin' on the dude you was askin' about ..."

"Which dude?"

"That guy you had been busting everybody's balls about."

"Bartkowski."

"Yeah, that's the dude."

"What do you have?"

"Is it worth $200 to yuh?"

"Maybe. Depends on what you've got."

"I might have seen him."

"Where?"

"Is it worth $200?"

"It is if I see him too. Now tell me what you've got."

"A white guy, fittin' your description, has been asking around for a 9 mm. I watched him 'bout 10 last night. He bought two 'heaters' from a brother I know. Afterwards, I followed him to the Blake Hotel. When do I get my $200?"

"If I find him, and he's Bartkowski, you'll get the money. I'll let you know."

Chapter 26

Coles quickly arrived at the Blake and sat in an obscure high-backed leather chair in a corner, overlooking the front desk and main floor restaurant. He had a Chicago Tribune and opened it and held it just low enough to observe the sparse traffic in the hotel lobby.

He was turning a page in the sports section, pretending to read a story, when he noticed a door opening from across the room. An average-sized, muscular tanned man emerged from the men's restroom. He hurriedly walked past Coles and disappeared down the stairway leading to the lower level.

Coles thought he recognized Bartlett, so he got up and followed down the stairway. Inside the old wooden phone booth next to the elevator, Coles observed the same man making a call. *I know he's Bartkowski.*

The street level was quiet and uninhabited, not surprisingly for this time of the morning. Coles approached, hid around the corner and waited.

A moment after leaving the phone booth, Bartlett felt the barrel of a gun in the small of his back. "Put your hands behind your head..." Bartlett considered his options. He had none. He clasped his hands behind his head.

Quickly and expertly, he felt the man's hand on his body frisking him up and down.

"Now turn around slowly," said the man. And, to his surprise, upon turning he was facing David Coles.

There was almost a smile on Coles' face. He remembered the look on Coles' face when they loaded him into the helicopter in 'Nam. And he remembered the moment their eyes met after the Brezinski assignment.

"I sort of hoped I wouldn't find you, Bartkowski. But now I have and we need to talk."

Coles put his revolver back in its holster. "Sorry about that...I didn't know how you'd react. You might be dangerous...Don't do anything stupid. I'd hate to have to shoot the man who saved my life."

The almost smile was back on Coles' face.

"Let's walk."

"You look good Coles. Being a cop must agree with you."

"Yeah. I joined the force after I got out of the hospital. I had a lot of time to think. I was on my back for four months. There were times when I wasn't sure I was glad you saved my life...but we don't have time to reminisce, Bartkowski. I'll get right to the point. I should arrest you right now for killing Brezinski. Not that the sonuvabitch didn't deserve it. I guess I'm not surprised that you're still killing people. You were good at it then -- I guess you still are now."

Bartlett remained quiet.

"This isn't the kind of reunion I wanted to have with you. I've always wanted to thank you. I tried to find you after I got out of the hospital but you seemed to have disappeared after your discharge. At this point, I don't want to know where you've been or what you've been doing."

"No thanks necessary. I just tried to help."

"I owe you one. But I'm glad to see you are in a hotel. 'Cause that makes me think you'll be leaving Chicago and that you live somewhere else. Don't ever come back to Chicago. If I ever see you again, I'll arrest you. That's the way it has to be. Understand?"

Bartlett nodded.

"I'm sorry our meeting had to be like this, Bartkowski. It seems like we're on different sides now..."

We're part of the same game, Bartlett thought to himself.

"Now get the fuck out of here. I don't ever want to see you or hear about you again."

"Thanks Coles, I appreciate it," Bartlett said. Feeling lucky, relieved and grateful, he quickly headed to his room, retrieved his bag and departed the hotel. Outside, he hailed a cab and got in.

"Where to?" asked the cabbie.

"The old cemetery on Farwell. I need to make a stop there. And then O'Hare."

"So you doin' some travelin'?"

"Just drive," said Bartlett, and handed the cabbie a $50. He was suddenly very tired.

As Coles disappeared around the street corner, he thought, anybody other than Bartkowski. *What a great collar he could have been. Well, he saved my life and now I have saved his. My debt has been repaid.*

Chapter 27

Detective Toussaint reviewed the file on SC Marketing as he had many times before. He knew Clements, Aguilar and Gentry were connected and perhaps Curtin, too. He promised himself he would put the pieces together and collect the reward from Aguilar.

Almost a year after the SC Marketing blaze, Clements' rip-off of Aguilar was still a popular topic in the New Orleans drug scene. The story was well known to everyone: Aguilar had personally helped to beat Gentry's brains out when he refused to give up Clements. Both Gentry and Clements were regarded as minor heroes for screwing the maniacal Aguilar.

Toussaint admired the caution Clements had used in establishing SC Marketing. The paper trail from the business was a series of dead-ends. Clements had carefully covered his tracks to and from New Orleans and Toussaint was certain that the business records destroyed in the fire wouldn't have yielded any more information. Adela Curtin, the only person who might have provided some information about Clements and his activities, was a charred corpse. "Emery Clements" had been very clever indeed.

Toussaint had only a few scraps to deal with. His inquiries to the Chicago police revealed that the phone number Curtin had written down was for "JBS Consulting," a personnel consulting firm which had been closed overnight. He knew not to expect detailed business records from JBS Consulting, and he was not surprised to learn from the Chicago police that a guy named Frank Russo seemed to be the principal behind the business.

Russo, who had few mishaps with the police, claimed he had opened the office to meet women and to interview women as models for nudie magazines. He had run several ads in local underground newspapers for models, but apparently not many had applied.

Russo's phone records interested Toussaint. There were calls to a local answering service and several long distance calls to Lehigh Acres, a small southwestern Florida town. The Florida phone had been activated and deactivated by Paul Stewart, an unknown to Lehigh officials. Stewart had rented the property for a short time and had disappeared from the Wyoming Street residence, leaving no forwarding address.

The Chicago authorities couldn't prove anything illegal had occurred at the office, other than Russo's failure to apply for a city license. Russo said he had been in touch with a man in Florida. They assumed Stewart was the man Russo was trying to help get a job. Strangely,

Russo failed to remember Stewart's full name. The police had interviewed Russo and then dismissed him, even though they sensed he was involved in some minor type of criminal activity. What type of activity, however, they couldn't prove or determine.

Toussaint had the Chicago police research the name Bartkowski, a common Chicago-area name. They discovered 20 Bartkowskis were currently residing in the metropolitan area. Interviews were conducted with all the Bartkowskis, but none seemed to be connected to Clements, Russo or Gentry.

On a hunch, based on the presence of the charred travel brochures, Toussaint checked with the Virgin Island police concerning Clements or Bartkowski, but there was no record of either person residing on any of the three Caribbean islands.

After checking and double checking all the leads, Toussaint was now beginning to realize Clements or Bartkowski or whomever had vanished, almost without a trace. If he could somehow connect Gentry, Curtin or Russo to Clements, then he could pursue the investigation further. But two of the subjects were dead and the other appeared unrelated.

Besides, the deaths of a drug dealer and a shoddy, small-time P.I. were of a lessor priority than those investigations involving mostly respectable citizens of New Orleans. The prosecutor's office wasn't exactly clamoring for a resolution to the case. They didn't even seem to care. Toussaint had been told by his captain, "You better hurry up, detective, and complete the goddamn investigation. I've got more important things for you to do than waste time on this crap."

So, as far as his superiors were concerned, Toussaint had closed the case file on SC Marketing, months earlier. But Toussaint secretly had been investigating on his own time. He planned to visit Russo, his only active lead, in Chicago, on his upcoming summer vacation. He would get more information out of Russo than the Chicago police had managed. Toussaint prided himself on knowing how to make uncooperative subjects talk.

Chapter 28

An artistically drawn billboard advertising the Riverside Hotel in Saugatuck, Mich., caught Bartlett's attention as he sped north on highway 131. The advertisement reminded him of the secluded motel where he and Moira had stayed on a vacation trip to the Lake Michigan shore. They had shared memorable times there.

He recalled a previous visit to Saugatuck, when they had embarked on a day-long shopping spree which began in South Haven and ended in Holland. They had spent several hours browsing through the specialty shops in the quaint little village, nestled near the river. He remembered the rustic eatery overlooking the water and he remembered seeing expensive powerboats and sailboats docked at the piers.

Bartlett pondered his decision to stay in Saugatuck, close to his assignment. *My presence won't create any unusual attention. Saugatuck is a tourist area and new faces are usual. I will be intermingled with the tourists. I should be fine here.*

He could stay almost unnoticed in one of the many bed and breakfast inns or small motels in Saugatuck. He knew it was the busy season there and he realized he might have trouble finding a place. He would take a chance, stop at several inns near the waterfront and inquire about a room. *Who knows, I might get lucky. Sunday night is probably the best time to find a room, if any are available.*

Before Saugatuck, Bartlett pulled into a gas station, relieved himself and purchased a Saugatuck street map. He was certain Lake View Drive would not be hard to find. As he suspected, the map showed Lake View was the closest road going north and south, nearest the Michigan shore. Bartlett shoved the map inside his pocket for future reference. He got back in the car and drove a short distance until he saw the main road leading downtown to Saugatuck.

The illuminated "no vacancy" signs were everywhere as he slowly cruised toward the waterfront. Next to the river, he stopped at the Riverside, a small two-story hotel. He parked and entered the building through a dimly-lit front portico.

Behind the counter, an attractive young blond woman greeted him politely and said, "May I help you sir?"

"Maybe," Bartlett said, giving her a playful glance. "Do you have any rooms left?"

"Oh, I wish I did," she said, "but we've been sold out for weeks. Your only chance is to pray for a cancellation tomorrow, but I doubt if we get any. We rarely do. Have you tried elsewhere?"

"No, you're the first. Could you recommend somewhere else?"

"Well ... this time of the year it's almost impossible to find a room in Saugatuck. How long will you be staying?"

"I'm not sure how many days I'll be in town."

"Well, your best bet might be to find a homeowner who routinely rents rooms."

"Where do I find them?"

"You can try the real estate shopper," she said, as she reached under the counter, grabbed the small advertising paper and handed it to him. "Here you are... it's worth a try."

"Thanks," Bartlett said, as he turned and casually surveyed the outdoor pool area on his way out the door.

Inside the car, Bartlett opened the paper and found a rental advertisement which read, "One room, neat and clean. Near shore, public beaches and shopping. Apply in person at #8 Lake View Drive." Bartlett pulled out the map and easily navigated to the location. *Interesting. My business would not be far from this rental.*

*   *   *

A "Room for Rent" sign was posted on a stake near a

small wooden walking bridge adjacent to #8 Lake View Drive. Bartlett parked the car and approached the narrow bridge, which would take him across a small ravine and up to the white, one-story home. The fragrance of flowers filled the air as he passed several bushes near the walkway. The home sat atop a cliff and was surrounded by ivy, flowering planters and tall trees. The location provided a beautiful panoramic view of the shore, a small nearby beach and an inlet. The inlet must lead back to town, he thought. Bartlett noticed a relatively new addition, which was added to the home. He assumed it was the property being advertised for rent.

Bartlett approached the main house and knocked on the screen door. A small, well-groomed middle-aged man with tinted rectangular spectacles suddenly appeared and greeted him after the third knock. "May I help you, sir?"

"Yes," said Bartlett. "I'm here about your room for rent. How much and how long will it be available?"

"The rent is $100 a night and it includes freshly-washed towels and sheets and a continental breakfast," the man said, beaming at Bartlett. "You can have it for two weeks, but I have someone else scheduled to move in afterwards. Will that work for you?"

"Yeah, I think it will. I'll take it."

"Wouldn't you like to see the space first?"

"No, it will be fine. I'll pay you for a week in advance."

"Oh, heavens no, that won't be necessary. Just pay me

when you depart. It's never been a problem before. I'm sure you won't cheat me," he said with a grin.

"No, I won't cheat you," Bartlett said. "Here's for one week," handing the man cash.

"OK, I'll take it...thank you," said the man. "My name is Stanley Kennedy," extending his hand.

"Paul...Paul Stewart," Bartlett said, as he shook Kennedy's hand. "Can I move in now?"

"Yes, the room is ready and cleaned. I've even put some fresh flowers in a vase on the dresser. If you need anything else Paul, please let me know."

"Sure...thanks," Bartlett said, as he carried his bag in from the car and began to unpack. Bartlett left the tool kit and equipment locked inside his suitcase. *This should work out fine.*

After unpacking his clothes, Bartlett decided to go on a leisurely walk to orient himself to the area. Walking east away from the lake and, after 10 minutes, he came to a river on the opposite side of Saugatuck. Across the river was a small park and in the distance was the town's business area.

A small passenger ferry, driven by an underwater chain system, was nearby at the river's edge. He imagined it was still operational. Next to the ferry there was a sign with an arrow pointing left to Oval Beach. He noted a dirt, two-lane road leading to the beach through a winding, wooded area.

Bartlett spent the next hour walking on and near the shore line road. He strolled past 315 Lake View Drive and noted the sounds of male and female laughter coming from the front screened-in porch. He was impressed by the well-maintained stately home. *Nice place.*

Several indistinguishable figures, which he assumed were his targets, visibly moved inside the porch. He stopped, tied his shoe and pretended to be admiring the wonderfully landscaped home.

It was almost 9 p.m. when Bartlett decided to conclude his activities, find a place to eat and then go to bed. It had been a long and stressful day. He was surprised and thankful that Coles had let him go, but he was disappointed that he had been so easily found. *Maybe this is a wake-up call. I'm making serious mistakes. I'm relieved this is going to be the last job.*

Chapter 29

Bartlett drove downtown and located a funky, main street tavern he had spotted earlier in the day. He parked in a bank lot near the bar. It was close to 10 and the usual Sunday evening crowd had thinned.

A flamboyant young woman, seated with a group of jetsetters, glanced at him when he entered the saloon. She looked enticingly attractive, he thought. The two young men she was seated next to were involved in an intensely noisy discussion concerning Michigan football. Their tone seemed to escalate as he walked by their stools.

Bartlett selected a secluded booth near the back exit. He noted, a slight hint of stale smoke, beer and grease upon entering the bar. He sat down and picked up a menu. Almost immediately, a perky, overweight waitress appeared to take his order.

"What you havin', hon," she asked.

"Ah…, I'll have a draft and a cheeseburger with pickle and mustard."

"I'll be back shortly with your beer…food will take 10 minutes or more," she barked.

"Great," he said, giving her half a smile.

A minute later, she set the beer down in front of him and Bartlett quickly took a gulp before he pondered the assignment.

Bartlett thought it odd Wallace had not yet decided on Stroh's fate. He wondered what his transgressions had been. Bartlett knew it didn't really matter, and he was being well paid to do the work. It was his last assignment. *What do I care?*

After the last couple of jobs, Bartlett found himself wondering about the reasons for the assignments. It was silly for him to imagine his clients explaining their requests to him. It had been a long time since he had remembered himself wavering back and forth with ideals.

Years ago, he had other lofty thoughts prior to his departure for Vietnam. The politicians had justified the conflict with the North Vietnamese as a way to stop communism in the region. The domino theory was part of the debate. The country and the soldiers were convinced the war was necessary and justifiable.

After his arrival in-country, he was soon cognizant of the nonsensical nature and hypocritical components of that war. Ever since, he had developed a distrust and hatred for the politicians who had sent him and countless others into the throes of combat.

God, more than 50,000 of our soldiers died and

thousands more wounded.

Bartlett considered himself one of the casualties of the war. Upon returning from Vietnam, he stayed in the shadows, feeling ashamed, isolated and betrayed. The mood in the country had changed and Vietnam veterans were made to feel unworthy of the honors and medals that were bestowed upon them. Bartlett had been given a medal for saving Coles, and he received the other usual service medals, too. At the time, those medals seemed irrelevant. He began to openly participate at public events with the hippies, long hairs and war protesters who he had hated before he went to Vietnam.

He had taken various jobs and could not find anything near the excitement of combat. The feel of a weapon under his control and his almost innate ability to kill made him want to become a professional "hit man." In fact, the act of killing had become acceptable to him after the war.

A neighborhood buddy and veteran, who he had known since school, introduced him to a "made" guy who gave him a first contract. Within two years, Bartlett had become a credible independent and his career blossomed from there.

But slowly and over time, and with the love of Moira, he had begun to feel a change smoldering within himself. Maybe that was his reason for caring; he didn't know. Strangely, he began to wonder about the relevance of his career.

The waitress returned and interrupted his thoughts.

"Excuse me hon…did you want fries with the sandwich?" she asked.

"No," he said with a frown.

"OK…sandwich is ready, I'll bring it out now."

She could sense he was thinking about something other than food. She placed the sandwich in front of him, along with the bill. "Let me know if you need anything else."

He didn't respond.

She turned and left. As he bit into the juicy burger, Bartlett began to think about the assignment again. His first priority in the morning would be to identify Louis Stroh and Anne Bishop. He intended to carefully watch them and learn their daily habits and peculiarities.

Bartlett assumed he would be allowed several days to prepare if Wallace ordered the hit. He would have preferred to know, up front, who he was killing and whether or not it needed to look like an accident. He knew things weren't always so smooth and simple. Complications were part of the business.

Bartlett's thoughts drifted toward the targets and their surroundings. Stroh and his girlfriend were staying in an older home, atop a large 100-foot cliff overlooking the Lake Michigan shore. There were desolate areas up and down the Michigan shoreline, not far from Saugatuck. Bartlett surmised Stroh probably owned a boat. The nautical chart on Lake Michigan that he had copied from the library indicated the water there reached depths of

100 feet a mile off shore.

Bartlett hadn't been in town more than a few hours and already he had some strategies for Stroh's demise. The final plan would need to be multi-faceted and well timed.

He thought it would be wise to plan for simultaneously disposing of both Stroh and his girlfriend. She could be deleted from the plan easier than added at the last minute.

He pondered some possible options: rigging an explosion involving natural gas, tampering with a hot water heater's exhaust vent or a small fuel leak, creating a vehicular or marine explosion.

He could murder Stroh and his girlfriend at the home, move their bodies to a remote site and dispose of them in a sandy, shallow grave.

Bartlett thought a mock burglary attempt run amok would be preferable over the prior scenario. Stroh probably didn't have a bodyguard or an alarm system to be concerned about.

He wasn't certain Wallace would want their deaths, no matter what, to appear accidental. He could conclude this assignment very quickly.

Bartlett knew arranging for an accidental death always required more planning, was riskier and more complex. He liked the challenge and the money he got for the work. He would be sure to remind Wallace about a price increase if the girlfriend needed to be included.

After dinner, Bartlett left the bar and decided to take a

short drive and acquaint himself further with the area. Winding streets and small roads were prevalent in Saugatuck. The village of Douglas was across the river, but the two towns bordered at several points. Other than in downtown, their residential streets were not well lit and both were sleepy little places.

Bartlett understood he could easily be the typical tourist, blend into the surroundings, complete the assignment and then disappear without attracting any undue attention.

The police force was small and probably very inefficient. They patrolled occasionally but he knew there wouldn't be much crime in Saugatuck or Douglas for the police to worry about. It was a small tourist community, perfect for shoppers, boaters, fisherman and fun seekers. He imagined an occasional drunk or a speeder might attract a cop's attention.

After the brief drive, Bartlett decided to treat himself to some dessert. He stopped at an old-time ice cream parlor and ordered a cone. Near the front of the store, a small child with a dripping cone attracted his attention. Bartlett smiled at the anxious, young mother who was wiping away the mess from her child's chin.

Peripherally, down and across the street, he could see window shoppers at a small boutique. He glanced in their direction and almost immediately turned and nonchalantly backed away from the brightly-lit street lamp.

Standing behind a small tree, he turned and peered

back across the street. Bartlett looked past the shoppers and toward a lone female who was casually walking toward him. He hoped his action hadn't attracted much attention and that the female hadn't been looking at that moment.

Bartlett turned and tried to conceal himself as the two couples and the lone woman stopped directly across from him. Strangely, the lone woman seemed familiar to him. Bartlett began to feel nervous and yet excited about her presence there. *She resembles Moira. Her mannerisms, shape and features look similar. Her casual stroll was similar, too. My God, what if it is her? What would I do, if she recognized me? Her presence would really complicate things. God, I'm on an assignment.*

Bartlett was feeling beads of sweat forming on his brow. It had been a long time since he had seen Moira and he wondered if she still cared for him. He never stopped caring for her. What would he do if the woman were Moira?

Bartlett decided to follow her and get a closer look to verify if she was Moira. As she paused briefly to window shop again, Bartlett realized the woman was Moira. She had changed her appearance slightly but she looked nice. She wore a newer hair style and she was wearing a colorful, silky dress that emphasized her figure. As she briskly walked across the moonlit street, Bartlett was becoming increasingly excited as he stared at her shape.

Bartlett watched as she approached the Riverside hotel, where he had been several hours earlier. Seconds later, under the portico, she turned, looked back toward the street and disappeared inside the hotel.

Bartlett stared at the portico almost in disbelief wondering when and why she was in Saugatuck. *I will need to be extra careful now.*

Chapter 30

Bartlett quietly returned to #8 Lake View. He could see the faint light of a flickering candle as he approached the house. He could hear the familiar notes of "Stardust" being played by piano, softly broadcast about the property.

Through a rear rectangular window, he could see the silhouettes of two people sitting closely on a piano bench. They appeared to be conversing and, as he approached near the back of the house, he could see Stanley Kennedy, his landlord, and a moderately attractive woman partially disrobed sitting next to him.

He watched as Kennedy removed his shirt and draped his arm slowly around her back. He could see the woman was wearing an alluringly tight black-laced brassiere. Her small but adequately-sized breasts were bulging inside the bra.

As Bartlett watched, Kennedy began to lightly kiss her lips, her neck and her bulging breasts. He was embarrassed. Generally he didn't make a practice of peeping through windows unless it was for business. This evening had been purely accidental.

He wondered if Kennedy or the woman could sense someone was watching as they began their lovemaking. Maybe the couple had seen the car pull up and had planned the performance for a spectator's benefit as well as their own.

He wondered why Kennedy had not been more discreet, knowing he had just taken on a new renter. His earlier thoughts and concerns about Kennedy's sexual preference had now been addressed. He knew first impressions were not always accurate. Things were hardly ever as they seemed.

Bartlett quietly walked past the picture window toward the rear of the home. There was a large screened-in porch overlooking the lake. He continued until he was dangerously close to the edge of the cliff. A trace of moonlight illuminated the sandy beach below and he could see for several blocks up and down the shore.

He wondered if the cliffs were as high in front of the Stroh house and if the shoreline consisted of rocks or sand there. If Stroh were drunk one night and enjoying a stroll near the cliff, an unexpectedly abrupt push from behind would be enough to propel him to a sudden death. It probably would be viewed as a tragic but accidental death. If his intuition was correct, Stroh probably drank more heavily while vacationing at the shore. It would be a simple scenario to orchestrate and an easy way to complete the assignment.

Bartlett was sleepy. It was 12:30 Monday morning. He needed to get a good night's rest and he hoped that tonight his demons would cooperate.

He pondered the assignment intently as he looked out upon the moonlit lake. Then he proceeded back around the house to his room. He unlocked the door, turned and peered back through the visible picture window. The bench was now barren and the couple had apparently departed for another room in the house. Quietly, he closed the portal behind him. Moonlight illuminated the room enough for Bartlett to easily find the bathroom and then a chair where he neatly placed his clothing.

He had traveled from Chicago to Saugatuck and now, in the early morning hours, he realized how difficult it had become. He was exuberant and at the same time anxious because of Moira's sudden and untimely appearance. Lying in bed, Bartlett closed his eyes and imagined he was back in St. Croix. Through the open window, he could hear the familiar and rhythmic motion of the waves crashing to the shore and then rolling back to the sea.

In the background, he could hear the sounds of soft music playing and an occasional voice from inside the house. The music and the voices hardly disturbed him as he drifted asleep.

The pleasant thoughts of Moira once again were stronger than ever as she had re-emerged back into his life. He wondered if he would ever be able to share his past life completely with her. He wondered what she would think if she knew the real Bartlett. The knowledge about his past career might be too much for her to accept.

He was sure his retirement would subject them both to plenty of risk. Not many paid killers were ever able to walk away from their work without consequences. It was generally a life-time occupation. In order for him to quietly end his career and retire in a tropical paradise, Bartlett knew he would have to be very lucky. But he had made a lot of his own luck before and somehow he had managed to escape disaster. Most professional killers either get whacked by others or they get caught and spend the rest of their lives in jail. Neither option sounded good.

As Bartlett slowly drifted to sleep, the ever-present nightmares of Vietnam were awakened within him. He was back in the Army and he was in Vietnam. He had just received the news about his mother's passing. He was scheduled to go home the next day. There was a big truck and he was riding in the back of it as it roared down the highway. The truck was headed for Tan Son Nhut air base and the familiar whine of the diesel engine was almost relaxing to him. All of a sudden, the sounds of small arms fire directly in front of the truck scared him back to reality. He ducked down for cover on the bed of the truck, grasped his weapon and readied himself for combat. The highway was well-traveled and patrolled, but convoys were always subject to hostile sniper fire.

As they sped up and quickly passed by a crashed Army Jeep on the right hand side of the road, he could see smoke roaring out from under the hood. A lone soldier was sitting in the driver's seat, slumped over the steering wheel. The jeep had been traveling directly ahead of their truck and the driver had become another unlucky recipient of hostile fire. The soldier had probably died instantly. As the truck sped past the Jeep, he could see a large jagged hole plainly visible through the back of the GI's head. Blood and flesh were interspersed inside the damaged and badly-smoking vehicle. It was another harsh reminder of the dangers of being in a combat zone.

Bartlett instantly was awake, sweating and lying rigidly in the bed. He listened for a nearby enemy to appear and then realized he had been awakened by yet another dream. *Mom's red scarf worked for me again.* Eventually, he slowly drifted back sleep.

Chapter 31

At daybreak, Bartlett awoke and made a small pot of coffee. He splashed cold water on his face and washed the sleep from his eyes. The water was refreshing and the coffee was beginning to wake him completely.

He was rested, but his sleep had been interrupted by another intense dream about Vietnam. When he returned from his tour of duty, he imagined that over time the nightmares would eventually end. He had been partially right. They had become less of a frequent visitor to his dreams, but they still arrived like an irritating mother-in-law making a visit.

He wondered again, when his career was ended and when his battles were finally done, if the dreams would permanently go away. He hoped so. He desperately wanted a normal life, devoid of his past.

Bartlett yawned and stretched his arms over his head. He was still awakening. Another cup of coffee and the usual morning jog would get his adrenaline flowing. A half hour later, he was out the door and jogging.

The Stroh house was several blocks away and he wanted to go to the house and have a quiet, undisturbed, lengthy look at the property. He assumed Stroh and the girlfriend would still be in bed. He couldn't imagine they would be outside gardening. Silly, he thought. Stroh was wealthy and probably had a service to care for the lawn, flowers and plants.

Most of the homes on Stroh's street had manicured lawns, looked grandiose and were new or well-maintained. He supposed most of the neighbors, like Stroh, were wealthy and prosperous. Bartlett imagined many of the properties were probably vacation houses, like the ones on St. Croix. He thought it would be very expensive to own a home overlooking the Lake Michigan shore.

Bartlett was grateful for his St. Croix home. He thought his view of the Atlantic Ocean, the trade winds and the consistently great weather was more preferable than Lake Michigan, particularly in the winter. He hoped he could quickly conclude his business with Wallace and go home to St. Croix, where he planned to retire. But he had a big problem.

At first, Wallace's assignment appeared to be relatively simple compared to the other contracts he had performed. The unexpected appearance of Moira Gray had become a real concern and he hoped her presence wouldn't hinder his ability to complete the job.

He had always imagined his final contract would involve a series of complex twists and turns, with a climactic ending, similar to the grand finale of a fireworks demonstration.

He was worried about the assignment. Its fulfillment appeared to be more complex than he had previously anticipated.

Bartlett understood he needed to be aware of Moira's presence in town and flexible enough to follow Stroh if required. He had disguised himself before coming to Saugatuck, with round, wire-rimmed glasses and he colored his hair brownish red. He decided to wear a University of Michigan football cap to help change his appearance further. He hoped not to run into Moira because she might still recognize him, regardless of his disguise.

This assignment could end up being more time consuming, and more dangerous, than any I have undertaken before. Worrying about someone else's welfare had never been an issue. He had always worked alone. Moira was unknowingly involved, whether he wanted her to be or not. An unplanned encounter with Moira would create a huge problem. She couldn't have come to Saugatuck at a worse time.

He wanted to see her, be with her and love her. But not right now. Their reunion would have to wait until sometime after the assignment was completed.

Bartlett's mode of operation was to locate the target, do the hit and depart without leaving a trace. It had never been that big of a deal for him. He was not an expected visitor. *Wallace has gotten this thing all fucked up with his indecisiveness.*

He considered contacting Wallace, explaining the situation and ending the assignment. His sense of duty wouldn't allow it; he had never left a job undone. He wasn't going to do that now. His professional reputation was at stake and he wanted to end his career, without a blemish.

I'll find a way to finish this work. Besides, if I don't finish the job, I'm not sure if Wallace could find another qualified hit man, at this late date. Wallace was only a front man, hired to make the arrangements. There was someone else more important than Wallace who wanted Stroh dead. Killing Louis Stroh would be a delicate matter and he was sure that is why they hired an independent.

Usually, there were lots of criminals eager to handle simple problems for their bosses. This was not a simple job. Stroh was a state senator, the current majority leader and a well-known Michigan politician.

Bartlett wondered if Wallace had hired others to monitor Stroh. He wouldn't doubt anything an attorney would be capable of doing. Wallace might have Stroh's home, office and car bugged. Bartlett had experienced this type of meddling before.

At first, most clients are skeptical about outsiders and particularly the ones they don't meet in person. He had never needed to defend his actions or his reputation. He was a very capable professional killer.

Bartlett had always assured himself the murders he had committed, were justifiable and necessary under the circumstances. In truth, until Moira, he really didn't care who he killed or why they needed to die. It was a job, just like Vietnam had been a job.

If Wallace wanted Stroh or anyone else dead and was willing to pay, normally it would have been alright with him. Bartlett had been devoid of any conscience for quite some time. But he felt like he was beginning to change, maybe wanting to change and he didn't quite understand the meaning.

Wallace's attitude was not very comforting. Bartlett didn't like putting himself at any unnecessary risk. He would need to work carefully to hid his identity and avoid detection.

Bartlett knew men like Wallace and his employer could be very dangerous. As he jogged, he wondered if Stroh had any preconceived notion of the dangers he faced.

The politician had evidently become a very serious threat to the man Wallace worked for, and that is why they called me. I know how to eliminate threats.

Bartlett had no knowledge that the attorney had little or no experience in dealing with criminals. High-end attorneys were generally known to be very capable and devious. Clients were always careful when arranging for assignments, but, up until now, he had never needed to wait for a decision. Wallace had acted a bit too premature and, Bartlett thought, his indecisiveness was foolish.

The light fog out on the lake was slowly dissipating as he neared Stroh's home. He noticed the early morning dew glistening on the lawn as he stopped, pretending to tie a loose shoelace. Slowly, he looked up and quickly made mental notes about the property.

Suddenly, the sight of a tall, distinguished looking grey-haired man walking down the front stairs, startled him. The man waved and gave a slight nod. Bartlett looked away and resumed his run. *The man must have been Stroh.* He wondered if the girlfriend would come out next. He looked back and saw the man disappear around the house. No one else was on the porch.

I'm thankful he didn't come over to say good morning.

Chapter 32

The cottage door squeaked as Stroh quietly opened the front door. Anne stirred in bed upon hearing the annoying sound. The room was darkened and she felt for his body, soon realizing Stroh was no longer next to her in bed.

The old house creaked and squeaked more frequently now if someone moved inside, making it harder to sleep. Stroh always tried to be considerate early in the morning not to disturb her on his way out. Sometimes either the doors or the creaking wooden floor would occasionally awaken her.

Normally, Anne slept soundly, but she was worried and concerned for Stroh's welfare after the secretive meeting transpired with Wallace. She could tell Stroh was worried, too. She knew there was a serious problem. Something was drastically wrong and she intended to find out what was bothering him. She wanted him to share the good and the bad with her. She had very carefully crafted their relationship, but his unwillingness to talk about the problem had Anne questioning his trust in her.

She decided, upon his return from the boat, she would be more insistent. She would ask for a further explanation concerning the meeting. She knew it had something to do with the casino legislation he had talked about. Stroh's skill in being able to push difficult bills through the Legislature had become his trademark. His leadership style and arbitration skills had given him the current Senate role. Anne wondered why he was so visibly troubled with Wallace and the Detroit casino legislation. Stroh worked hard and she knew he would eventually get the legislation passed. She couldn't understand the sense of urgency associated with this legislation. She was aware that he had already made numerous calls to key members of the Senate in order to solicit their support.

It was so unlike him to mix business with their pleasure. She didn't like it and she wanted it to end. *This business could just wait until the vacation was over.* She considered telling him the sexual favors were postponed until he either offered an explanation or concluded the casino business.

Stroh walked down the front steps and headed for the unattached garage near the rear of the home. As he stepped onto the sidewalk, he caught a quick glimpse of a lone jogger bent over tying his shoe. The jogger was looking in his direction, seemingly admiring the house.

The cottage, as Stroh called it, was in good repair and he was proud of its appearance and placement amongst the finer homes on the shore. He wasn't surprised people stared at the property. Surprisingly, the jogger failed to speak and quickly looked away as Stroh smiled and attempted a short nod of acknowledgment. The runner was not local, he was sure. The locals always spoke and waved at him. There were many out-of-town visitors in Saugatuck during the season and many jogged past his home and down the shore road. Shore road was a relatively quiet street, which afforded runners a safe and scenic course to enjoy for an early morning run.

Stroh decided this morning to do minor repairs and some routine maintenance tasks on the boat. Just before noon, he would drive home, clean up and have lunch with Anne. They had made plans for a shopping spree later in the afternoon. Maybe he could talk her back into the bedroom after lunch. Maybe she would be willing to postpone the shopping until another day. He thought the prospect of another session of love-making was more appealing than shopping.

When Stroh pulled out of the driveway, Bartlett had stopped and watched him drive away in his fancy red Cadillac. He presumed Stroh was headed for a morning breakfast meeting.

On his return jog past the house, the sight of a shapely and attractive woman in an upstairs window, caught Bartlett's attention. He assumed the woman was Anne Bishop, the girlfriend, that Wallace had mentioned. He thought it would be a shame if he had to kill such a lovely creature.

Across the street from Stroh's house there was a series of wooden steps extending from the top of a steep cliff to a rocky shoreline below. Bartlett stopped, sat on the ground next to the steps and removed a shoe. He pulled up one of his socks and intently glanced back at the house and the woman. He stared for several minutes and then arose and continued to jog toward the river and the marina.

Down the hill, Bartlett saw the red Cadillac parked in a large, nearly empty lot. He jogged down the winding road, which he discovered was the entrance to the marina. He stopped and pretended to catch his breath at the bottom of the hill.

Haley's Marina consisted of a large main building nearest the water used to house a small ship's store, a boat maintenance area and bathroom and shower facilities for slip renters. Outside there was a large trash bin near the back of the building. There were several other larger building for boat sales and storage up the hill. The owner had recently been developing condominiums with slips included for sale. Haley's had several hundred rental slips utilizing three long piers extending out into the Kalamazoo River. Sail and power boats were randomly moored on both sides of the piers. Two boats were outside awaiting sand blasting and one was being bottom painted Bartlett noted, as he approached the building.

He went inside the ship's store, hoping to find a boat owner's directory indicating their assigned slips. The store had shelving with snacks, boating accessories and personal items. A soft drink machine was outside next to the front door. Near the entrance to the maintenance area there was a large, inconspicuously placed bulletin board with names colorfully posted in red and green.

He glanced at the board and found Stroh's name written in red. According to the roster, Stroh's boat was moored on pier A, slip #159.

"What's red mean?" Bartlett casually asked the young preppy female clerk as he stared at the sign.

"Red is sailboats and green is power boats," she stated. "Are you looking for someone?"

"No, just curious about the colors," he said as he turned and headed for the door.

"Can I help you with anything else?" she asked.

"No, but thanks," Bartlett responded.

Chapter 33

When Bartlett exited the store, the three front piers commanded his attention. Pier "A" was located to the far right and a hundred feet from the building. The long, grey metal pier mostly had large, expensive sailboats moored on both side of the structure.

A pristine looking white, yellow and red sailboat near the middle of the pier caught his attention, as did the man who was emerging from the cabin. Stroh, wearing a blue-striped shirt and khaki shorts, was easily visible from the shore. Bartlett watched as he began hosing down the hull.

He had considered walking out on the pier to get a closer look at Stroh and the elaborately-rigged vessel. He thought getting so close might not be a good idea. Instead, he decided to watch from a partially-secluded park bench, located under a large willow tree. He looked at Stroh, the sailboat and the marina and realized he needed to familiarize himself with all three. Across the river, Bartlett could see the Saugatuck business district and the small hotel where Moira was staying.

Under the tree, Bartlett felt comfortable, safe and relaxed. He briefly closed his eyes and imagined himself back in St. Croix. The long and droopy willow branches moving gently in the breeze sheltered him from view like an overprotective mother holding her young. The weather is perfect for boaters and fisherman, he thought. What a great day ... calm seas, cool breezes, hot temperatures and almost no humidity. *It doesn't get any better than this.*

Bartlett knew Saugatuck was a great place during the summer to vacation. When he and Moira had stayed there, they mostly ate, shopped and sat by their poolside room. Under other circumstances, he would have liked to cruise the river and the lake. Maybe he'd have chartered a small fishing boat. However, the assignment required his complete attention. He had little time, because he expected Wallace to change the plans almost any day. He needed to be ready and he needed more information about the residence and the couple.

Stroh's Cadillac, a grey Mercedes convertible, several other cars and a lone, white van were the only vehicles in the large, marina parking lot. The van was parked conspicuously at the far end of the lot. Bartlett walked onto the asphalt and headed toward the entrance to the marina complex. As he neared the entrance, he saw a large man sitting in the van. Bartlett questioned what the man was doing. Generally, employers would not want their employees sitting around and wasting time. Maybe the man was taking a mid-morning break or a nap, he thought. As he strolled by the van, Bartlett looked at the driver, smiled and said, "Good morning." The man nodded and returned a slight but forced grin.

The driver, a burly, olive-skinned, middle-aged man casually dressed in a Detroit Tiger's shirt, appeared to be staring in the direction of pier "A." He was talking on a cell phone as Bartlett approached the van. He thought he heard the man say something about signal clarity. When Bartlett passed by the van's open window, the driver went silent with the phone still at his ear. Bartlett noticed he was wearing a fancy watch, a gaudy golden ring on his right pinky finger and a large gold chain with a crucifix around his neck. He wondered about the man's occupation.

The vehicle was an old, late-model white work van. Defreeze Electric, Grand Rapids, Mich., was shown in faded black lettering on the side. As Bartlett passed the rear of the van, he turned to momentarily check the Michigan plate. He would remember the driver, the license number and the vehicle.

As Bartlett jogged back toward Lake View Drive, his thoughts temporarily drifted away from Stroh, the man in the van and the assignment and shifted back to Moira. It was a shame he couldn't be with her now, he thought.

Arriving back on Lake View Drive, his thoughts returned to the assignment. If Wallace wanted Stroh killed, Bartlett decided to kill them both outside the home. He didn't know if Wallace would want the bodies disposed of or not. He wasn't sure if Wallace would want their deaths to appear accidental. First, he would need to get into the house and check it out. He would have to be quiet, cautious and professional to avoid detection.

At the completion of the assignment, he decided it would be wise to check out of his rental room. Bartlett didn't want his departure to attract any undue attention. He would tell the landlord he was being called away on business. He would be like the typical tourist, reluctantly leaving after an enjoyable stay in town. Within hours of doing the job, Bartlett wanted to be out of Saugatuck and headed back to Chicago.

Bartlett approached the corner home, next to Stroh's residence. He stopped to wipe his brow and catch his breath. There were tall, clumped and fully blossomed flowering bushes across the narrow street from Stroh's neighbor. Bartlett stopped to smell the flowers. He sat down on the curb and positioned himself next to the thick plants, relaxing momentarily.

Looking downward, the lake appeared calm, bright blue and pristine. On the opposite side of the bushes was a staircase leading to a secluded sandy beach below. The beach was vacant. Bartlett stared down at the water and noticed a small power boat, slowly cruising north right off shore. He could see the passengers and hear an occasional laugh coming from the vessel.

Nonchalantly, Bartlett got up and moved to the lake side of the plants, safe from Stroh's nosy neighbors on the other side of the street. Periodically, he would turn around and look away from the water toward Stroh's home. He hoped the house would be easy to get inside. He wondered if there were any unlocked windows at the rear of the home. If not, he was proficient with picking locks. The existing home lots were separated with tall, thick bushes between the houses. Their foliage would easily hide a lone intruder at night. The constant humming sound from nearby air-conditioners and fans would cover any forced entry sounds, he thought.

It was almost 11. No sign of life in the Stroh home or at the neighbors. Occasionally a vehicle would slowly pass the house and disappear around the corner toward town. Bartlett began wondering if the girlfriend was home. Maybe she'd gone shopping while he was watching Stroh at the marina?

Bartlett's inquisitiveness was soon answered when a good-looking blond emerged from the home and was standing on the front porch. She had on a white terry cloth beach coverup and underneath, she was wearing a bright red bathing suit. Bartlett had not seen her face, but she looked like she had all the curves in the right places. He couldn't fully appreciate her beauty. When she approached and crossed the street, he could see her face and her body. He noted she was a beautiful, well-proportioned woman, tanned, with high cheek bones and long, wavy blond hair. Bartlett imagined she knew she was beautiful, too.

He watched as she descended the wooden stairs leading to the water and the beach below. He followed her every move as she unfolded the chair, removed her cover-up and got into the water.

Bartlett enjoyed the view for about 30 minutes before seeing the Cadillac pull into the driveway. Stroh emerged and entered the house. His attention had been shifting alternatively from Anne to the house. A half-hour later, Anne climbed the stairs and disappeared back inside the home.

He was pleased at 1 o'clock when the couple emerged and headed for the garage. He imagined they were, probably going for lunch. Bartlett waited several minutes before he briskly walked to the rear of the house. He tried opening several rear windows, but they were locked. The back door was secure but Bartlett easily picked the lock and entered the house.

There was a long hallway leading to the front of the house through the pantry, kitchen and dining room. A large stone fireplace accented the elegant living room, entryway and the adjacent main floor study. Upstairs, there was a large master suite and three other bedrooms located on the opposite side of the home.

In the master suite, Bartlett discovered a small "transmitter" placed inside an artificial planter atop a dresser. The white van probably contained the audio receiving equipment, he thought. He had suspected Stroh and the girlfriend's activities were being monitored. *Bartlett wondered if Stroh ever suspected anything?*

The view of Lake Michigan from the master suite was gorgeous, but similar to his view in St. Croix. Bartlett stared briefly out the window and his thoughts drifted back to the safety and serenity of the island. He sighed, knowing this would be ... his last contract.

When the white van from the marina slowly passed by the home, Bartlett knew it wasn't there to make any repairs. *Probably the guy is a private detective but he looks like a thug, Bartlett thought. Time to go.*

Quietly, Bartlett descended the stairway and carefully secured the rear door behind him. He wanted to leave the residence quietly and untouched without compromising his presence to the residents or the man in the van. Bartlett quickly walked down the stairs and disappeared in the dense woods behind the house, allowing himself a safe exit.

Chapter 34

Monday afternoon the heat index had risen to an uncomfortable level. Inside the van it was hot and humid. The driver, Tony Cavallaro, was sweating profusely. Cavallaro, a distance cousin to Ricci, was disgusted with the assignment.

He wondered why he couldn't have driven a vehicle with air-conditioning and why he had been given the job. He was tired of listening to Stroh and the woman all the time and he was tired of being in the van. After all, he was a soldier for the Riccis, not a private detective. His job was to keep others in line, not be the next Sherlock Holmes. Two more days of this shit, he kept telling himself, and then someone else takes over.

Cavallaro decided the sonovabitch Wallace probably had recommended him for the job. He couldn't understand why Ricci listened to Wallace. The guy was weak when you get him out of the courtroom ... and he wasn't Italian. He didn't have the guts for business.

Cavallaro wondered why they hadn't gotten a private

detective for the assignment. He was tired of playing Holmes and tired of listening to Tiger baseball on the radio. Besides, next to red wine and pizza, baseball was Cavallaro's passion. He had great seats behind the Tiger's dugout, main section, row seven. Already he had missed several games because of the assignment. This is bullshit, he thought.

Cavallaro finished his Coke, checked his watch and decided to contact Wallace, with a daily up-date. There was nothing new to report, but he needed to check in. He reached for the cell phone on the passenger seat. It's portability, range and clarity still amazed him. He dialed the number. Cavallaro thought he'd ask Wallace if he could switch to another vehicle – one with air-conditioning and a better radio.

"Hello," Wallace answered.

"Yeah, this is Cavallaro."

"Anything new?"

"No, nothing to report. I'm waiting for them at the house."

"Where are they now?"

"Out to lunch ... been gone half hour or so. They talked about sailing afterwards."

"Did you get a boat?"

"Yeah, no problem."

"Have you noticed anybody hanging around the

marina or near Stroh's home?"

"No. Should I be looking for somebody?"

"Well ... no. I'm just being cautious."

"Oh…this morning a guy walked by my truck at the marina," Cavallaro said laughingly. "He smiled at me and said 'hi.'"

"Have you seen him again?" Wallace responded, sounding slightly troubled.

"Hell no."

"Good. But if you do, I want to know."

"Sure, I'll get his name ... maybe introduce him to you later."

"I'm serious!"

"Look the guy was queer, OK."

"Well, OK, but if he shows up again, I want to know."

"Yeah, sure. But, don't get so fuckin' excited."

"I don't need complications."

"What can go wrong? I'm only listening and watching them."

"You're right. What's Stroh been doing anyway?"

"You mean besides screwing the woman?

"Yes."

"She's a moaner."

"Really, what else?"

"He's been cleaning his boat," Cavallaro said. "Is there any chance I can get relieved early?"

"No," Wallace said sternly.

"Can I use my car for a while instead of that piece of junk?"

"You got to be kidding me. Workmen drive trucks and vans, not luxury cars. Just do your job."

"Yeah, OK."

"Good," Wallace said as he hung up the receiver.

*   *   *

Five o'clock in the evening, Wallace decided it was time to update Ricci. He wanted to assure him the surveillance effort was working well.

"It's Wallace."

"Yeah I know. What's happening with our friend?"

"Well, we've bugged his boat, house and car. He still seems stable since I met him for dinner in Holland. He seems understandably nervous, since I brought up his girlfriend."

"He ought to be."

"He hasn't mentioned the photos or anything specific

about our meeting to her yet. He appears still willing to cooperate. I'm not sure his assistance will be enough to pass the legislation this session."

"Counselor, it better be, if he knows what's good for the two of them," Ricci said.

"I know."

"I've warned that motherfucker plenty of times. I even had his wife killed, unbeknownst to him, so he could avoid the divorce and collect the insurance."

Oh my God, thought Wallace.

"He'd better produce or that is it," Ricci said sternly. "Let's continue the surveillance and keep Cavallaro there indefinitely. Keep me posted."

"Yes, sir," said Wallace as Ricci hung up the phone.

* * *

Wallace sat back in his chair and took another gulp of scotch. *I can't believe he killed Stroh's wife.* Suddenly, he was fearful for Stroh's life and maybe his own. He was aware of Ricci's impatient nature. He couldn't understand Ricci. Stroh's ongoing services would be very useful to the Riccis in the future, regardless of the casino bill.

He wondered again if Ricci would be upset if he found out about the "consultant." Ricci hadn't given him any instructions to hire an independent yet. Wallace knew

Ricci wouldn't have to know about the "contractor" as long as everything worked out. Wallace hoped the consultant's service would not be necessary. He hoped he could find a way to make Stroh understand and to convince Ricci to accept whatever happens with the casino legislation. It would be better for everyone.

He hoped Cavallaro wouldn't get in the consultant's way. If anything bad happened to Cavallaro, there would be consequences. Cavallaro was one of Ricci's favorite cousins. Wallace was nervous. He reminded himself about the consultant's employment condition concerning "absolute anonymity" once on assignment. He hoped he wouldn't have to explain Cavallaro to the consultant. He'd have to work around him. He assured himself Cavallaro wasn't going to be a problem.

*   *   *

After Bartlett departed the Stroh home, he decided to double back and observe the van parked conspicuously, down the street. There were thick flowering bushes adorning Lake View Drive next to the vehicle. Bartlett crossed the street a block away and maneuvered himself through tall bushes and trees to within 10 feet of the vehicle. He was close enough to smell the driver's cigarette smoke and to see his head and shoulders.

Bartlett positioned himself near the ground on the other side of the hedge row next to the van. The occupant was talking on a cell phone and he could hear the deep voice of the driver saying ...

"I just spoke with Wallace about five minutes ago ... nothing new here to report. It's damn uncomfortable though. Tell Ricci I'll call him later."

Bartlett wasn't surprised when he heard the name Wallace. He had suspected surveillance. He understood employers wanted first-hand verification on his work. *Another reason to never trust employers, he thought.*

Lack of mutual trust was prevalent in his line of work. He wondered about Ricci. Was Wallace working for Dominic Ricci, the crime boss of Detroit? Bartlett had never worked for him before, but he understood the man was ruthless in business although he respected loyalty.

Bartlett needed to call Wallace in the morning. He'd be surprised if the surveillance guy or Ricci were mentioned. *He thought, if Wallace tells me about the surveillance guy in the van or his boss Dominic Ricci, I might be more willing to trust him.*

Chapter 35

It was late Monday evening and Bartlett had eaten a quick sandwich earlier at a roadside diner outside of Douglas. After dinner he returned to Saugatuck, drove past Stroh's house and again checked out the neighborhood. Stroh's home was dark, the garage was empty and the white van was no longer in sight.

Upon returning to #8 Lake View, Bartlett parked his car near the wooden bridge and briskly walked to the room. The landlord's house appeared empty and his car was gone. Bartlett thought his absence was a welcome sight. He knew it was best, while on assignment, to keep personal contacts as infrequent as possible.

Bartlett checked his belongings, including the kit, and put on a black running outfit. He took a short nap and waited until it was dark. Then, he jogged back to the Stroh residence to resume his watch.

He positioned himself at the wooden stairway across from the home. Only half of the properties on the street, seemed inhabited. Stroh's place looked dark and deserted.

The afternoon downpour had reduced most of the intense heat, but the night air remained humid. The warm and sticky atmosphere of the Michigan shore reminded Bartlett of his home in St. Croix.

It was 10:30 when the red Cadillac pulled into the drive. Louis and Anne emerged from the garage and headed up the steps, arm-in-arm, to the screened-in front porch. A minute later, the familiar white work van quietly stopped down the street. The driver quickly doused the lights and turned off the motor.

Bartlett could hear laughter and sometimes muffled conversation coming from the porch. He assumed the man in the white van was listening to the couples conversation. And very clearly, he thought.

Bartlett checked his watch, again. It was 11 o'clock and the couple was still awake. He wondered when they would go to bed and if this was their normal routine.

At 11:30, the lights were extinguished downstairs and Bartlett could see a light through an upstairs bedroom window. He assumed it was the master suite. Several minutes later, the house was dark and quiet, except for the humming noise of the air-conditioners.

Down the street, Bartlett could see an occasional glow of a cigarette coming from inside the van. He wondered how long the van would stay at the home. Undoubtedly, the man would be listening as long as the couple were awake. At midnight, Bartlett departed for his rented room.

*   *   *

Inside the van, Cavallaro was getting fatigued. He had been watching and listening all day. He was tired of hearing Stroh and tired of his constant line of bullshit. Once they were in bed, he hoped they would screw and quickly fall asleep. He wanted to go back to the motel for a few hours of needed rest.

*   *   *

In the master suite, the couple had just gotten into the king-sized bed. They lay in each others arms, gently nestled together. Stroh knew he was more fatigued and tired since his meeting with Wallace. Tonight he felt like he would be able to peacefully drift asleep. He had kissed Anne and said "good night." His sleep seemed only moments away. Anne broke the silence and startled him by saying, "Louis ... tell me what's troubling you."

Stroh waited for several moments and then nonchalantly responded, "Anne ... it's really late. Everything is being taken care of ... it's practically over ... nothing to worry about now."

"Louis," Anne whispered softly into his ear.

"Yes," he said softly.

"I'm glad it's over."

"Me too," he said, beginning to feel relaxed again.

"But, honey," she said. "Please tell me what has been going on? You haven't been yourself lately."

Stroh decided to comment briefly in an attempt to satisfy her curiosity by stating, "I received several favors from Wallace and I needed to repay him."

"You mean the casino legislation?"

"Yes."

"What were the favors?"

Disappointed in her continued persistence, Stroh responded, "Anne, I'm really tired. We can talk in the morning. Alright?"

"No. I want to know now," she said, with a hint of conviction in her tone. "What are you hiding from me?"

"Nothing."

"I know you are keeping something from me. This is the first time I've ever felt left out of your life. I don't like the feeling."

By now Stroh was getting disgusted and puzzled by her insistence on pressing the issue, so he said, "Look ... we'll talk in the morning. OK?"

"Louis, I've always been honest with you ... please be honest with me," she said, almost pleading.

Stroh paused and became silent for several seconds. Then he said, "I took money from Wallace. In return, I was supposed to pass the casino legislation. As you know,

I have run into some trouble."

Anne gasped. "What are you going to do?" she asked.

"I've tried everything I know, but timing is the problem. I'm sure I can get the bill passed but it will take more time. Wallace apparently doesn't believe my sincerity. I've told him to be patient. He has begun to apply pressure and threaten me."

"Are you in danger?"

"Not really. I think they're merely trying to bluff me. I will tell Wallace to lay off or else I'll talk to the authorities. They won't do anything to me. They need my services."

"Who else is involved besides Wallace?"

"His boss," said Stroh, who was wishing he had never told Anne anything by now.

"Oh. Who's he?" asked Anne.

"Anne, really ... I've got things under control. Now, I've told you about my problem. Let's go to sleep. Alright?"

"I'm really worried about you Louis," she said softly.

"See why I didn't want to tell you," Stroh said.

"Yes, but I have a right to know. I care about you."

"Thanks for caring about me, you're sweet, but it's not necessary for you to worry. They will play it my way or else I will talk to the authorities," Stroh said sternly. "I know how to handle these kind of people. Believe me."

"Thanks for trusting me, Louis. I love you," she said, kissing him lightly on the lips.

"I love you too," Stroh said, as he kissed her forehead, rolled over and snuggled up against her body. "Now, let's go to sleep," he said.

"OK," she whispered.

*　　*　　*

The phone rang several times before Wallace answered the call. "Hello," he said.

"This is Cavallaro."

"What's up?"

"Stroh just got done telling his girlfriend about the casino deal and the money. He said he would talk to the authorities if you didn't back off and stop threatening him. He said he knew you were bluffing and he knew how to handle you."

"Did he mention your cousin's name?"

"No."

"Good."

"What do you want me to do now?"

"Go back to the room and get some sleep and I'll call you in the morning."

"OK. I'll wait to hear from you," Cavallaro said, as he put the phone down and started the van.

*   *   *

Wallace thought for several seconds and then decided to call Ricci.

"Hello," said Ricci.

"It's me ... Wallace. Sorry to bother you this late but..."

Ricci interrupted, "It's OK, what's going on?"

"Our friend talked to his girlfriend tonight. He told her we were bluffing. He said he planned to threaten us if necessary if we didn't lay off him. He said he would go to the authorities. What do you think?"

"I'm not surprised," said Ricci. The motherfucker. His kind are all alike. They think they're invincible and beyond our reach."

"What do you want me to do?"

"Get an independent and take care of them both. Pick someone from the list I gave you. They are all reliable..."

"Are you sure you want to handle it this way?"

"Don't question me," Ricci said angrily. "Just do it and right away."

"Sorry, I was just ..."

"Just make the call. This is what I pay you to do."

"Also, is my cousin still there?"

"Yes, how did you know he was ..."

Ricci interrupted him again, "Good. Afterwards, have him take care of the independent, too."

"The independent," Wallace responded. "Are you sure?"

"Yes, just do as I say. Alright?"

"Yes, OK."

"Good night then," said Ricci. "Call me in the morning."

*   *   *

Cavallaro had just gotten out of the shower and was about to get into bed when the phone rang. He answered the call and was surprised upon hearing Ricci's voice.

"Tony, are you awake?"

"Sure, what do you need?" Cavallaro asked.

"We are going to hire an independent for Stroh and his girlfriend. Wallace will be calling to tell you. Wait until after the independent has done his work, then take care of him. Understand?"

"Yeah, no problem. I'll take good care of him."

"Tony, listen carefully. I want you to meet with Wallace later this week after our business is finished. Tell him to meet you at the warehouse, right off 75. He knows the place. He has screwed up some important things and I'm not sure he can be trusted. I don't want his services anymore. But nothing messy. OK?"

"I'll take care of everything," Cavallaro said.

"I'm relying on you. This is very important to the family and to me," said Ricci.

"Don't worry, I know what to do. I'll call you when it's done."

"Keep in touch," said Ricci.

Chapter 36

As Bartlett started the rental car, he heard a sputter, a cough and saw a cloud of smoke visible in the mirror. Damn rentals. They are generally reliable, but you could get a bad one, he thought. It would not be good to have a problem now. He put the car in gear and checked his watch. It was Tuesday morning, almost 8 o'clock. He would phone Wallace promptly as instructed.

When he stopped at a sign, he squinted his eyes, yawned and stretched inside the vehicle. He hadn't been able to sleep soundly the last several nights. The assignment and the nearness of Moira in Saugatuck had caused him to be overly anxious.

Bartlett was equally distressed about the continued presence of the burly man in the surveillance van. He was sure Wallace would say, "The man was there only to monitor Stroh." He thought he had made it very clear to Wallace in their initial conversation about his condition of absolute autonomy. Either Wallace was setting him up or Wallace was incredibly naive to ignore his warning. He would discuss the surveillance problem in their forthcoming conversation.

After driving around the fringes of Saugatuck to kill time, Bartlett pulled into a roadside convenience store to call Wallace. He walked to the telephone mounted outside on the building and dialed the number. He was pleased when the attorney quickly answered the call.

"This is the consultant," said Bartlett.

"Morning," said Wallace.

"Have you decided anything?"

"Yes. You can take care of the two of them."

"When?"

"As soon as possible."

"Do you want it to appear accidental?"

"I don't think that will matter. Just take them somewhere and get rid of the bodies."

"OK, I'll work on it, but I think I've seen a place that will work."

"Fine. Just get it done soon."

"OK, you remember the balance of my fee is due upon completion," said Bartlett.

"Agreed, but I'll need proof."

"Proof!" Bartlett responded. "What kind?"

"Easily recognizable proof!"

"That was never part of our deal."

"How else will I know it's been done?"

"My reputation speaks for itself."

"Fine, but I still need proof."

"It's never been needed before. What's the reason?"

"This is our first time with you."

"So what?"

"I've got a job to do and so do you."

"Then maybe you ought to get someone else."

"No. I want you for the job. You came highly recommended."

"Well then, what's the problem?"

"Look, just get me proof. Anything believable will work."

There was a slight pause and then Bartlett said, "What about the surveillance guy? I told you I worked alone. It makes it harder for me to do my job."

"He's not there on my authority. You'll have to work around him."

"That's not my usual procedure."

"Don't worry ... he's harmless."

"I'm not worried, Bartlett said coldly. "Where did you get him."

"He works for my boss."

"Really, for a P.I. he is not too professional," said

Bartlett.

"He's not a P.I."

"Oh, what does he do for your boss?"

"Look," said Wallace, quickly avoiding the question. "We've paid you and ..."

Bartlett interrupted and said, "OK, but I want the balance due in cash, $50s and $100s, in exchange for the proof."

Wallace paused again and said, "I had anticipated wiring the money to you. How will we get together?"

"I'll call when I'm ready."

"OK," said Wallace reluctantly.

"Just make sure you have the money! I want to leave right after I've completed the job."

"OK, that's fine."

"I'll be in touch."

After ending the call, Wallace hung his head and sat motionless in his chair, pondering what he had just done. He was in way over his head and he knew it. Ricci had sucked him all the way into the family business. He had never imagined himself being involved like this before. The consequences of his actions made him almost sick. Ricci knew what he was doing, and now so did Wallace. There was no choice. Stroh was getting killed, regardless. Wallace hoped by handling this problem he would be able to regain his credibility and redeem himself with Ricci.

Otherwise, Wallace wondered if he would be next.

*   *   *

It was almost 9 when Wallace got Cavallaro on the phone.

"Why didn't you answer your phone?" Wallace asked.

"I was in the bathroom," Cavallaro responded. "I didn't hear the phone ring."

"OK. There has been a change of plans."

"Oh yeah!"

"I've ordered the job on the pair, but keep listening and watch out for the independent. I want you to stay as far back from Stroh as possible. Give the independent plenty of room so he feels safe. Understand?"

"Yep."

"Listen to me. When you can verify the assignment has been completed, follow the independent and take care of him. But be careful. He is very ingenious and he knows who you are."

"Don't worry. The guy will have to show himself sometime before he does the job. I'll be ready."

"Be sure. Your cousin doesn't want any mistakes."

"I understand. I'll take care of it."

"He will be doing his thing tonight, probably after they

retire. When it's done, he says he is going to contact me for the balance of the fee. He wants to meet me somewhere near Detroit. He said he'd call but he didn't say exactly when. I figure he'll call in the morning. That's all I know. OK?"

"Have you ever seen the guy before?"

"No, but his voice sounds strong and yet he seems very subdued."

"The guy won't be a problem."

I hope you're right Wallace thought as he hung up the receiver.

* * *

Bartlett located a pharmacy and then a hardware store in nearby Holland to pick up some needed supplies. He decided to stay clear of Saugatuck until later in the day to avoid running into Moira. He would check out of the room shortly after noon and go to a desolate beach buggy place not far from Saugatuck. He would wait there until nightfall and formalize his plans.

He decided after he dealt with Stroh and the girlfriend, he would drive to Detroit and contact Wallace the following morning. He would meet Wallace, get his money and then return to Moira's home in Evanston to wait for her.

He hoped Wallace wasn't planning anything stupid in

regards to the payoff. He didn't like being double-crossed. He had warned Wallace twice about the condition of absolute autonomy. He wondered what the burly man's real job was if he wasn't a P.I.

Bartlett was beginning to smell a rat and he didn't like it. *Did Wallace think the guy in the white van would be able to retrieve the payoff money from me or muscle me?* He decided to deal with the burly man first before he did anything with Stroh. Wallace had probably lied to him and, if so, he would deal with Wallace and his boss, too.

Bartlett parked several blocks from the Stroh home and slowly walked along the shore road. It was dark but he could see the shape of a car parked alongside the road, more than a block away. As he approached, he could see the silhouette of a large person sitting in the driver's seat. Cigarette smoke was rolling out of the vehicle as he neared the idling car. Bartlett sensed the driver was the same man he had seen before in the surveillance van. He snuck up and stuck a revolver through the car's open window, next to the driver's head.

"Don't turn around or I'll fucking kill you," Bartlett said. "Now open the door, so I can get in."

"Don't get nervous buddy ... I'll do whatever you say," Cavallaro said.

Bartlett reached around the driver and frisked him. He wasn't surprised to find a revolver in a holster under the man's left arm.

"What's this for," Bartlett asked.

"For protection. I'm a private investigator," Cavallaro said.

Bartlett knew he was lying. "Who do you work for?" Bartlett asked, pushing the gun harder in his ear.

"I'm on my own," said the man, now beginning to sweat.

"Really? Put the car in gear and drive toward the highway."

"OK," said Cavallaro. "Where too?"

"Just drive."

Bartlett was silent the whole way as the pair headed toward the sheltered beach area. "Pull in here," he said to the man as they approached the turn off.

Cavallaro noticed a sign that said "Dune Buggy Rentals, Weekends Only" just as he turned off the highway onto a sand-covered lane.

He wondered what this guy was intending to do with him. He'd wait and see, but he was worried. He couldn't believe he hadn't taken what Wallace had said, more seriously. He wasn't quite ready to die yet. "Hey buddy, what have I done to you?" Cavallaro boldly asked Bartlett.

"Shut up and stop here," Bartlett said.

"I was just watching the couple."

"Shut up, I told you," Bartlett said, jamming the barrel inside the man's ear.

"Don't hurt me. I got little kids," pleaded the driver.

"You'll be OK if you do as I say," said Bartlett, placing a rag drenched with chloroform over the man's mouth and face. Cavallaro struggled but Bartlett grasped him firmly and, within seconds, Cavallaro had collapsed in the front seat. Bartlett climbed over the seat and shoved the man toward the passenger's side.

He searched the vehicle and found a small box that resembled a radio. He was sure the device was some kind of radio receiver. An ear plug and line dangled from the device. A cellular phone plugged into the cigarette lighter lay on the floor.

Bartlett searched the man's clothing and found a lighter, a wallet and a golden money clip stuffed with large bills. He took the money clip, the wallet and the revolver. He looked at the wallet and saw the man's name was Tony Cavallaro on his driver's license.

There was a pair of handcuffs inside Bartlett's pocket which he used to restrain the man. He jammed a cloth inside the man's mouth and tied another cloth securely around his face.

A small metal building housing a dozen or so dune buggies sat 20 feet off the sandy pathway. The sign above the building read "Saugatuck Dune Buggies." Bartlett drove the vehicle through the opened overhead door of the structure and turned off the engine.

He grabbed the unconscious man and pulled him out of the vehicle. He found an old wooden captain's chair and placed Cavallaro in it. He used duct tape to restrain the man's arms, legs and body. Several minutes later he used an ammonia inhalant to awaken the man.

Immediately the thug flinched at the smell of the ammonia and awoke to an extremely bad headache. He noticed Bartlett was standing in front of him as he regained consciousness.

Almost immediately Bartlett hit him across the face and said, "What the fuck are you doing here?"

"I'm on a surveillance job that is all. Who are you anyway?"

"Don't bullshit me, I intend to find out right now," he said. And without blinking an eye, Bartlett pulled a large knife from his pants pocket and cut one the man's right fingers off. The man shrieked with pain.

Bartlett placed the severed finger inside a plastic bag and threw the bag on the ground. "Now tell me what you are doing or else I will cut all your fingers and toes off before I'm done.

"Jesus man, what are you doing?" Cavallaro said, grimacing with pain.

"Who do you work for and what are you doing here?"

"I'm on surveillance and I work for Henry Wallace. Hell, I don't know man. I'm just on the job, that's it"

"Listen asshole, I don't have much time and I am tired of listening to your shit. Bartlett located a small axe on the work bench and returned to Cavallaro and said, "If you want to keep this shit up, I'll cut your fucking hand off. Don't lie because I'll be able to tell," he said. Bartlett raised the axe over the man's hand and said, "We don't have to do it like this, but it's up to you."

"Ok … Ok! Cavallaro said. What do you want to know?" Within moments, he had answered all of Bartlett's questions.

"Thank you," Bartlett said, as he produced another chloroformed rag and placed it over Cavallaro's nose. The man went limp in the chair. Bartlett wrapped the man's hand with a large cloth and tied a firm knot around the stub of the severed finger. He knew the man would be all right because the business was open on weekends. He would be found in a few days.

Bartlett had seen lots of men survive worse injuries and under more adverse conditions in Vietnam. The guy would have a sore hand but he would survive. Bartlett knew Cavallaro would always consider himself to be extremely lucky. *I could have just as easily killed him.*

Once his business was complete in Saugatuck, he would first collect his money and deal with Wallace and Ricci later.

It was a four-mile jog back to Saugatuck and another mile and a half to the Stroh house. Bartlett placed the receiver, cell phone and the plastic bag containing the severed finger in his backpack. He placed the backpack around his shoulder and began a fast-paced jog toward town.

Chapter 37

After a 60-minute jog, Bartlett was winded and had stopped only once to catch his breath. He hadn't run this far in a while and he was feeling his age. Thirty-two years ago, he had been able to go for hours in full gear through mud, marsh and the rice fields of Vietnam. This assignment had required him to operate more on foot, rather than by car, which was something he normally tried to avoid.

Professional killers were skilled at their jobs, primarily because of their ability to adjust and adapt. Bartlett was no different. Even at 51, he was near the top of his game. He was still quick on his feet, bright and very creative. He had guts, no fear and his special skills would be hard to replicate.

When he departed, his knowledge of past hits would make him vulnerable. His departure would not be looked upon favorably by the mob. As he crafted his retirement, he knew it would take someone very skilled to find him. He was betting as time passed, they might never succeed.

If they ever did, he would be ready.

Bartlett cautiously approached Stroh's house from the woods behind the home. The moonlight shone brightly on the road leading to the woods and the yard behind the house. Bartlett could see the neighborhood easily, even though several tall pine trees partially blocked his view of the garage and Stroh's home. Cautiously, he walked near the property line, staying close to the bushes, toward the street. He wanted to see if there were other vehicles monitoring the home. He saw none and concluded the man in the van had been working alone.

The home looked barren from the outside, so Bartlett checked the garage. The Cadillac was gone. He couldn't see any activity or hear any sounds coming from inside. After several minutes, he decided to enter the house. He had been more cautious since the night Strawberry had entered his house. He didn't want or need any more surprises on this job.

The staircase leading to the upstairs bedrooms creaked as he slowly climbed the stairs. Ever resourceful and lucky, Bartlett was glad he hadn't entered the home while the couple was in bed. He was sure the creaky steps would have announced his arrival. Each step he took on the stairway offered a different but annoying sound. He wasn't worried about any other so-called "private detective." He doubted if there was another replacement for the burly man in the van.

Bartlett thought he would wait for the couple's return in an adjacent bedroom next to the master suite. A charmingly ornate, high-backed, upholstered chair sitting next to the window looked inviting. Bartlett sat down and stared out the front window toward the lake. The street was extremely quiet, even for 10:30, he thought. It appeared Stroh and the girlfriend were going to be out later than normal. He had anticipated their arrival at or near 11. The chair was comfortable and Bartlett found himself almost drifting asleep as he sat, patiently, waiting for their return.

At 11:30, lights shone brightly on the street and then illuminated the front yard as a car turned into the drive. It appeared to be Stroh, but he couldn't tell for sure until the car entered the garage. The opener light illuminated the inside of the garage and he could see Stroh and the girlfriend getting out of the car.

Bartlett could hear them talking as they entered the home. They were slurring their words and Bartlett thought they were both intoxicated. He hoped they would be too drunk to hear the small noises he might make when he entered the bedroom. Earlier, he had removed his shoes. He planned to walk in his stocking feet, which he thought would help limit further noise. It would be impossible to make no sound. He decided to go into their bedroom after he heard evidence both were sleeping.

Bartlett sat patiently through their simple conversation and preparation for bed. At midnight, a gentle snore was coming from the bedroom. He assumed Stroh was asleep but he wondered about the woman. He waited 20 minutes more before he decided to act. He arose from the chair and slowly walked into the master suite. The floor creaked as expected but not enough to wake the couple. He carried a set of chloroformed rags in one hand and his pistol in the other.

The moonlight illuminated the shapes of a man and a woman sleeping uncovered and backward to each other in bed. First, he approached the man and placed the chloroformed rag firmly over his mouth and face. The man struggled slightly but quickly was knocked out. He waited for a moment and placed the other chloroformed rag over the woman's face. She responded more violently, but her body surrendered to the pungent, sweet-tasting anesthetic quickly. He removed the duct tape from his bag and taped Stroh's hands and feet together. Then he did the woman's. He shoved another rag inside their mouths and secured them with tape.

A large diamond clustered ring was visible on Stroh's finger. Bartlett eased the ring off his finger and carefully placed it in a small plastic bag. He quickly searched for jewels on the woman's hands. There were none. A diamond ring, several diamond pendants and some jeweled clustered earrings were visible in a jewelry box. He grabbed the jewels and placed them inside another plastic bag. He shoved the bags back inside his pocket. Stroh's wallet contained several hundred dollars in cash. He quickly stripped the cash from the wallet and put the wallet in his pocket.

Bartlett carried the woman down the stairs and out to the garage. He quickly returned to the house and emerged almost immediately with Stroh draped over his shoulder.

Inside the garage, Bartlett tripped the latch on the garage door opener shaft and manually raised the door. He got inside the car and started the engine. The engine idled loudly until he lightly tapped on the gas pedal to slow the engine down. He backed the vehicle out of the garage and into the street and quickly turned north on Lake View Drive. Bartlett gradually sped up until he reached the intersection of the main highway. It was 1 o'clock. *So far, everything was going as planned.*

As he drove, Bartlett checked his rearview mirror to make sure he wasn't being followed. The highway was almost deserted with the exception of an occasional car or truck passing him, from the opposite direction. During their ten minute trip, Bartlett hardly saw anyone with the exception of several people pumping gasoline at a convenience store.

The sight of a badly-worn billboard advertising Ford trucks indicated to Bartlett he was close to his destination. A half mile later, he turned the car into a dark, narrow lane draped with overgrown bushes. There was an overturned sign near the entrance to the lane that read "House For Rent."

The lane led to a faded white farmhouse and a worn looking red barn off to the side. There was a clearing in front of the house and a dense woods behind the home. Bartlett placed a mask over his face and opened the trunk of the car. Inside lay Stroh and the woman. Bartlett shined a flash light on the pair, who were gagged and securely tied. They were obviously awake. It was evident they were consumed with fear. The woman had been crying and the man seemed near tears.

Bartlett helped Stroh out of the trunk and ripped off the tape from his mouth. He gasped for air and said, "Kill me but spare the woman. She is an innocent."

"Shut up and do as I say," said Bartlett.

"OK … OK … ," Stroh responded.

Bartlett closed the trunk with the woman still inside and led the man toward the woods behind the home. Ten feet inside the woods were two shallow graves. He threw Stroh in one of the holes and said, "Keep quiet or I'll kill your girlfriend."

The man nodded his head and began to weep. A minute later Bartlett returned with the woman and placed her in the other hole. He pulled out his 9 mm and pointed it first at Stroh. The sound of the gun firing made the woman hysterical and she began to shake. Then, he pointed the gun at her and fired. *My last assignment is almost complete.*

Minutes later he walked to the Senator's car, threw his kit into the trunk and drove away. Bartlett was tired but he had things to do before he could sleep.

Five hours passed and Bartlett placed a call to Wallace at his northwest Detroit residence. The phone rang and Wallace answered, "Hello."

"This is the consultant. It's done and I have your

proof."

"Did everything go well?"

"Yes."

"Good. Do you want to meet at my office later today?"

"No," Bartlett stated coldly.

"Well, where do you want to meet?"

"Meet me in Toledo, Ohio, Exit 4, at 4 this afternoon. There's a Holiday Inn not far from the exit. Check into the hotel under your name and I'll contact you there. Come alone. I'll be watching."

"OK. No problem," he said.

"Remember ... cash, $50s and $100s. Also, throw in an extra 10 for the woman."

"OK, I'll be there."

"See you this afternoon," Bartlett said as he hung up the phone.

Wallace got out of bed, turned on the light and sat up. He wondered if Cavallaro was ready to kill the consultant or not. He certainly couldn't tell if there had been a problem from the man's tone. After several minutes, Wallace called Cavallaro's cellular phone again. The phone rang but no one answered. He hoped Cavallaro would take care of the consultant like he had been instructed to do.

He was anxious to report the news about Stroh's demise to Ricci, but he would wait until after he saw the proof. *I hope Stroh's death will satisfy Ricci and redeem me. If everything goes as planned, I will owe Cavallaro an enormous favor.*

Chapter 38

Roşa liked it when Bartlett was gone because she received extra money for running the shop. She dreamed of the day when she would open a business of her own. She ran the daily operations, except for purchasing merchandise and paying bills, and the experience she gained was invaluable. She had proven her worth to Bartlett many times, and he was always pleased when she recommended merchandise to sell in the shop. Rosa was grateful for his confidence, the opportunity to learn and for the extra money.

Upon entering the shop, Rosa quickly readied the store for another business day. Thankfully, business was good the past week. Bartlett always seemed concerned when the shop didn't do well. Rosa suspected the shop wasn't his only source of income; small time shopkeepers, like Bartlett, didn't normally have fancy houses overlooking the shore. She was grateful for his generosity and trust.

She occasionally wondered what other business interests he had secured back in the States. She thought his mainland trips were not just for the shop, that some were for his very guarded personal affairs. She decided it would not be wise to pry into his life too much. Such knowledge about someone else's business could end up becoming a problem.

Bartlett's personal affairs were private and what she didn't know couldn't hurt her. She had sensed there was another side of Bartlett. Regardless, he treated her well, her employment status was stable and she needed to work. And her presence there afforded Bartlett the freedom to pursue his other interests. He appeared happy to have Rosa's ideas, which had enhanced and improved the business. Bartlett seemed pleased about the results and glad for the increased sales and profits.

While away, Bartlett always called the shop to check in with Rosa. The prior Saturday was no exception. She had reported no problems and sales were good. Several local artisans had stopped to sell their crafts. As usual, she reported to Bartlett that she had told them they'd "have to see the owner next week."

Habitually, he called Rosa about every third day. Wednesday morning, when he stopped to get gasoline at a roadside station, he noticed a nearby pay phone and made the call. The telephone rang several times before he heard Rosa's cheerful voice.

"Ursula Shop, Rosa speaking, how may I help?" she said.

"How are things going without me?" Bartlett asked.

"Just fine, Mr. Bartlett. It's good to hear your voice. I was just getting ready to sweep before you called," she said.

"How's the weather?"

"It's been quite hot. When will you be coming home?"

"I'm not sure yet ... maybe a week or so. Can you get by without me for another week?"

"I suppose ... but it's never the same when you're gone," said Rosa emphatically.

"Sounds like you're doing fine. I'll call again in a few days ... thanks Rosa," he said.

"I'll talk to you later. Goodbye," she said.

Bartlett hung up the phone and wondered how Rosa might react to Moira if and when she came to St. Croix. He hoped they would get along, but he didn't want them to become too close. The secrecy of his past life was part of his plan to secure a safe future. He would caution Moira about divulging anything she knew about his past work. Rosa might not always be so trustworthy.

He decided to tell Moira that "any talk about my past work would violate the terms of my contract with the U.S. government and would jeopardize our safety." He was certain she would understand and comply with his request.

*   *   *

Nine-thirty. Wallace had nervously gulped down his third cup of coffee and had smoked several more cigarettes. He had tried several times, unsuccessfully, to contact Cavallaro late last evening and early this morning. Wallace thought after about 12 hours Cavallaro should have answered his phone or contacted him. He was beginning to wonder whether Cavallaro had failed in his attempt to kill the consultant. If Cavallaro were dead, Wallace knew his life would be in jeopardy, too. The consultant would undoubtedly hold him responsible for Cavallaro's actions and so would Ricci.

Several more hours passed and Cavallaro still hadn't called. Wallace was extremely nervous, but he was thankful Ricci hadn't called either. He wouldn't know how to respond to the mob boss with no news to report. At noon, Wallace checked his office messages. There was no word from Cavallaro, only one message confirming an upcoming dental appointment.

I should have never trusted Cavallaro to handle the consultant. I heard he was good at knocking heads but I don't know if he should have been trusted to handle a skilled professional killer.

Wallace wasn't prepared to tell Ricci how to run his business affairs. He would only offer advice and, in rare cases, offer a strong recommendation. He regretted not speaking up more strongly about Cavallaro's weaknesses.

Cavallaro was related to Ricci and he would not have liked hearing his favorite soldier and nephew, Tony Cavallaro, was not capable of doing the job. Wallace knew the way to survive and continue working for a boss like Dominic Ricci was to be absolutely loyal to him and totally accept his decisions whether they made sense or not.

Ricci would be relieved to know Stroh and the girlfriend were dead once he received convincing proof of their demise. He was afraid to tell Ricci about why he had originally hired the independent. Wallace hoped he wouldn't need to inform Ricci that Cavallaro was missing and possibly dead.

If Cavallaro were dead, presumably killed by the consultant, Ricci would want to send someone else to go to Toledo with Wallace, to finish the job. Regardless, Ricci wanted the consultant dead, whether by Cavallaro's hand or by somebody else's. Whoever did the job, it would not matter to Ricci as long as it was done.

If Cavallaro wasn't dead, taking Ricci's men to Toledo might interfere with his plan to kill the consultant. Again, he reminded himself, the consultant had warned him to come alone. He said, "I'll be watching you." Wallace was certain the consultant, if he were still alive, would be watching and very closely.

Wallace phoned Cavallaro again. There was no answer. *Had Cavallaro taken care of the consultant already and forgotten to call? I doubt it. I wish now that I had asked Cavallaro for a tentative plan on when and where the job would be done. What a mess.*

He had not anticipated making the exchange away

from Detroit. If Cavallaro failed to contact him by 1:30, Wallace decided, he'd have to go to Toledo to meet the consultant, alone. At 2, he began to pack his bag with the cash. For protection, he would pack a .22-caliber pistol too. He had never fired on anyone before, but he would if it meant his survival. The consultant would probably never expect him to be a threat.

Strangely, Wednesday had been a quiet day in his office, and he was surprised Ricci hadn't called yet. At 2:30, he got into his car and began the hour-long trip to Toledo. Wallace pondered how the worst-case scenario might affect him. The consequences would be predictable and bleak if Cavallaro failed in his attempt to kill the consultant. A blunder would surely cost him money and perhaps his life.

He hoped for a better scenario. A scenario where Cavallaro kills the consultant before the payoff meeting occurs and saves him the cash. Regardless, he understood the consultant had to be eliminated. God forbid if he'd have to do the job himself. The thought of his direct involvement scared the shit out of him.

Wallace had no idea what to expect. He was anxious to get this business behind him. *If I get out of this mess with my life, it will be a goddamn miracle.*

Again, Wallace wondered about Ricci's response. He hoped Ricci would be pleased if the senator and the girlfriend were dead. He hoped this would allow him to save face and avert a potentially dangerous crisis. Wallace realized he would still have to find another way to get the casino legislation passed and without Stroh. The idea of getting another legislator to cooperate with the Riccis seemed easy now compared to his present predicament.

*　　*　　*

Bartlett watched for Wallace to arrive from an adjacent parking lot next to the hotel. It wouldn't be too hard to spot him going into the Holiday, Bartlett thought. He had studied Wallace's picture from a law directory he had accessed in the Chicago library.

It was a quarter till four when Wallace pulled into the parking lot. When he got out of the car, Bartlett recognized him immediately. Wallace opened the trunk and retrieved a small black bag, which he cautiously carried inside the hotel. He appeared nervous and reluctant when he approached the front doors.

Bartlett had surveyed the hotel, including the elevators and exits, hours before Wallace's arrival. He had been watching the hotel, the parking lot and the adjacent properties for the past two hours. If anyone looked suspicious, they would have immediately caught his attention. Bartlett noted the hotel guests arrived infrequently but the cocktail lounge seemed a popular destination for the locals.

Earlier, Bartlett disguised himself, using a short, neatly-trimmed fake beard. Hours before in a shabby roadside motel, he had dyed his hair and beard dark gray.

He wore silver-rimmed glasses and a double-breasted navy suit.

It was 4 and Bartlett crossed the lot and headed for the hotel side entrance. Inside at the front counter he found a pretty middle-aged woman fiddling with a computer as he approached.

Bartlett smiled and said to her, "Ma'am, I hope you don't mind, but you are a very beautiful woman. Are you as intelligent as you look, too?"

She blushed and then responded, "Well, I think I am."

"You are the very person I need to help me," he said.

"How can I help?"

"Well, I was parking my car outside the hotel about 10 minutes ago and I saw an old law school buddy of mine coming inside. I haven't seen him in years and it would be marvelous to surprise him. However, I don't know his phone number."

"Is he a guest in the hotel?" she asked.

"I presume so. His name is Henry Wallace."

"Well, let's see," she said, fidgeting once again with the computer. "Yes, he's staying with us. Would you like to talk to him on the house phone?"

"Sure, where is it?"

"It's around the corner," she said, smiling brightly. " I'll get the number for you."

"Oh," he said. "You know, it really would be great if I

could just knock on his door and surprise him that way."

"Well, I'm not supposed to give out room numbers ... but you look like a nice gentleman. He's in room 167."

"Thank you ma'am," Bartlett said. "He'll really be happy to see me. I won't tell anybody. I promise."

"I hope not," she said.

"I'll see you later. Thanks again."

"Have a nice evening, sir."

Bartlett walked around the corner and disappeared into the connecting hallway toward the room. He easily located 167 which was near the back of the hotel. Bartlett walked down the hallway toward the other side of the hotel. There he noticed a cleaning cart parked in front of a doorway to an opened room. Bartlett approached the cart and looked inside the room. Peering inside, he saw an older black woman emptying trash into a container. He quietly entered the room and gently closed the door behind him.

"Hi," he said. "Did you find my book on the night stand?"

The woman was startled and quickly turned to look toward the door. As she did, Bartlett removed his pistol from inside his belt and pointed it directly at her. She was shocked to see him pointing a gun at her and she was frightened.

"What you want wiff me, mister? I ain't got no monies, except for a few bucks."

"Just turn around and don't scream. I don't want to have to hurt you."

As she turned, Bartlett removed a roll of gray duct tape from his bag and began to bind her hands. He covered her eyes with a dark cloth and secured it with tape. Bartlett shoved another cloth into her mouth and taped it shut, leaving only her nostrils uncovered.

"I'm tying you up, but I won't hurt you, if you cooperate," he said. "I hate to have to do this, but I have to keep you silent."

Bartlett pushed her into the bathroom and carefully placed her on the stool. With duct tape, he secured her around the toilet. He turned the lights off and closed the bathroom door. Slowly he went out to the hallway and pulled the cleaning cart into the room. He removed the wall mirror, turned it around and placed it next to the wall. Bartlett ripped the phone wire from the phone and threw it on the bed. He went into the bathroom again and retrieved the maid's house key from her apron pocket.

Bartlett exited the room and headed for the house phone in the front lobby. He called Wallace. The phone rang once before the man answered.

"Hello …," Wallace answered, sounding very nervous.

"Have you got my cash?

"Yes. Are you in the hotel?"

"Leave the room in exactly five minutes and head for the lobby. And bring the black bag with you. I'll meet you there. For your sake, there better not be any surprises or else you will be dead."

Bartlett briskly walked toward Wallace's room and counted three minutes on his watch. At the intersection of the hallways nearest room 167 Bartlett stopped and waited for Wallace to appear. At exactly the five-minute mark, Bartlett heard a room door open around the hall and then quickly shut. Moments later, Wallace appeared at the corner carrying the black bag. Bartlett quickly grabbed him and turned him in the opposite direction toward the room where he had secured the maid.

"Don't turn around and walk normally," Bartlett said.

"No problem."

"I have a pistol pointed at your back. If you do exactly as I say, we can get this thing over as quickly as possible."

When they came to the room with the maid tied up inside, Bartlett handed Wallace the key and said, "Open the door and don't turn the lights on." As he entered, Bartlett quickly turned and looked down the hallway in both directions. They were alone and there was no sign of trouble.

Once inside, Bartlett frisked Wallace and was surprised to find he had armed himself with a .22-caliber semi-automatic. He grabbed the gun and put it inside his belt. "What's this for?"

"Protection," said Wallace.

"You're lucky I'm not shooting you with it right now,"

said Bartlett. "Don't move." He located the small table lamp on the dresser and turned on the light. "Is the $20,000 in the bag?"

"Yes. Where's the proof?"

"First things first. Don't turn around and slowly lie face down on the bed."

Bartlett reached inside his jacket and threw a small Ziploc bag with an object wrapped in paper on the bed. It bounced several inches and stopped on the edge of the mattress near Wallace's face. "Open the bag. The proof's inside."

Wallace opened the bag and saw an object which was covered with dried blood. He looked at it and then dropped the bag on the floor. "God," he said. "What the hell is this?"

"Recognize the finger and the ring? It's the senator's. I thought I'd bring you a little gift along with the proof."

"Jesus, what am I going to do with this?"

"Keep it as a souvenir. The woman's gone too. Shame, she was a real looker."

Bartlett opened the black bag and looked inside. He quickly counted the bills and shoved them into a small shopping bag he had brought. "Everything looks in order."

"What do we do now?"

"Well, I'm going to secure your hands and feet. Shut up and stay on the bed with your face down into the mattress. You will be able to untie yourself in several minutes," Bartlett said. "Just a precaution. Sorry." He picked up the phone line and loosely tied Wallace's hands and feet. "Stay here for at least five minutes. If you come out before then, I'll fuckin' kill you."

Then he flicked the table lamp off and headed for the door. Bartlett turned to have one last look at Wallace before departing. As he left, Bartlett again said, "Remember, wait five minutes before you leave this room." He opened the door and quickly closed it behind himself. His car was parked a minute away beside the hotel. Bartlett placed the money on the front seat, carefully backed out of the space and slowly drove out of the lot.

The Ohio Turnpike was less than a half mile from the hotel. Bartlett continued to check the rearview mirror for unwelcome visitors until he reached the Indiana line. He was relieved everything had gone well. He had the money and his task in Saugatuck was completed. He was ready to go back to Chicago and be with Moira again.

*   *   *

Wallace waited for what seemed like an hour before he got up from the bed. He quickly was able to untie himself. He turned on the small table lamp to illuminate the room. He noticed a cleaning cart partially shoved inside the clothes closet. The air-conditioned room was cool, but

Wallace was still perspiring. He had never been as frightened as he had been with the consultant. The sight of the finger and the absolute coldness of the man was eerie.

His throat was parched, so he opened the bathroom door to get a drink of water. When Wallace stepped inside, there was a stale odor dispersed in the room. When he turned on the light, he was startled to find the cleaning woman taped to the toilet. Her eyes, mouth and ears were covered with cloth and tape. The consultant must have really scared her, he thought. Not surprisingly, he realized, she had shit her pants.

After thinking about the situation for several minutes, Wallace decided to depart, leaving the woman behind still taped on the toilet. She would be found later, he thought. He didn't want to get mixed up in explaining what he was doing in the room. Wallace closed the bathroom door, picked up his bag and threw the Ziploc container with the severed finger and ring inside. He waited another minute to regain his composure and casually left the room.

He doubted if Cavallaro had a chance to kill the consultant. He probably never even saw the hit man coming before it was too late. Cavallaro was probably going to be found dead somewhere and he realized he probably would be next. His only hope would be if Cavallaro were still alive. He hoped Ricci would blame Cavallaro for the screw up, rather than himself. *Maybe Stroh's death will be enough to save me.*

Chapter 39

It was late Wednesday evening when Bartlett arrived in Chicago. Traffic had seemed excessively heavy for a Wednesday night on the Indiana Toll Road and on the expressways in the city. Bartlett dropped off the rental car at the airport and hired a cab to take him to Evanston. He got out of the cab a block away from Moira's residence and walked through the neighborhood to her home.

The house was dark and the garage was empty. He assumed she was still in Saugatuck on vacation. It seemed almost surreal to have seen her there. Now he was standing in front of her empty home. He was glad his business had been concluded quickly and glad she didn't get involved or in his way.

Bartlett felt on top of the back door casing and quickly located the spare house key. He quietly opened the screen door, unlocked the deadbolt and let himself inside the home. He was not surprised she hid the key outdoors. Occasionally, she would lock herself out of the house and need the spare. Bartlett had never known her to trust her neighbors; thus the need for hiding a key.

Inside the home, Bartlett smelled the familiar bouquet of potpourri in the kitchen. The several nightlights in the hallway were enough to illuminate the inside. Arriving at the bedroom, he pushed the door open and quietly peered into the room. The bed was unoccupied and he was not surprised to find the room completely in order. The closet door was closed, the bed was made and the usual decor of throw pillows, scented candles and lace adorned the bedroom.

Bartlett retrieved his luggage from the back porch and carried it into the bedroom. He took a long, warm, overdue shower, put on some pajamas and climbed into bed.

Before drifting asleep, he reminded himself of how lucky he was to have survived another assignment, without dire consequences for himself. His work was always dangerous and the men who usually hired him were capable of setting him up to be double-crossed or worse. Under the circumstances, Bartlett felt lucky the past assignment had gone well.

The lingering fragrance of Moira's perfume on the pillow reminded him of her. He missed being with her and he hoped she would believe his explanation and forgive him. He wanted to resume their relationship and he was in a position this time to make it last. The continuing thoughts of her consumed his consciousness as he slowly closed his eyes and fell sleep.

At 7:30 Thursday morning, the phone rang. Bartlett stirred in the bed but quickly got up, dashed to the kitchen and listened for the answering machine. After Moira's prerecorded message was played, he heard the voice of a woman say "Hi, Moira. It's Pauline. If you get back in time for dinner Friday night, give me a call. Hope is coming from Wisconsin, the grandkids are gone and you know how much I hate to eat alone. Well, call me if it's early. Bye." The message was important to Bartlett. It meant Moira was probably still on vacation and was not expected home until the next afternoon or evening.

Bartlett was pleased he could go back to bed and pleased to know approximately when to expect Moira. He debated whether or not to stay there for another day or to check into a motel. Either way, he decided his presence in her home and back in her life would be quite a shock. He knew she wouldn't have wanted him to stay anywhere else. She had said many times, "My home is your home." When he lived in downtown Chicago, they had stayed at her house more frequently than they had slept in his apartment.

It had been over a year and a half since he had been in her life. He wondered if she had been faithful to him. If she hadn't, he didn't need to know. Either way, he would never ask for an explanation.

At 10 o'clock, Bartlett rolled out of bed and treated himself to another warm shower. He was rested and relaxed. It had been a long time since he had experienced a restful sleep. He felt extremely safe in her home and in her bed. It was strange to be in bed without her. The only thing the home lacked was Moira. He hoped that situation would be remedied soon and his lengthy absence would eventually be forgiven and forgotten, too.

At noon, Bartlett left the house and walked several blocks to a local eatery for lunch. After dining on a sandwich and a beer, he found a pay phone inside the building and made a telephone call. He dialed FDR Consulting and heard the familiar voice of Russo on the answering machine. After the announcement, Bartlett said, "I'm moving. Close the shop for now. I'll send ample cash to cover expenses. The extra is yours. We'll be in touch." Then he hung up the receiver and walked outdoors.

* * *

Early Friday morning, Moira was awakened by the loud humming noise of a fishing boat idling, sometimes sporadically, at the charter boat pier next to the hotel. The usual sounds of morning activity on the river seemed amplified by the light fog and humidity. She arose early; it was her final day of vacation. She had enjoyed her stay in Saugatuck, but she was ready to go home. Around 11, Moira settled her account with the front desk and loaded the car. She slowly drove through the downtown area leading to the highway out of town. She thought of some memories she would carry back to Evanston while passing through the thriving little community. Fun memories of boating and swimming in the lake, trying on casual clothing in the boutiques, sampling ice cream and chocolates and dining in the finer restaurants in town.

It had been a restful, relaxing and enjoyable vacation, even though she hadn't made any new male acquaintances. Initially, she had thought it would be fun to play a little, but she decided she would wait for Bartlett. It had been a long time since his mysterious departure and absence. He would be back sometime soon, she hoped. He had left her with a great deal of money. Moira believed he would eventually reappear. And when he did, she would be happy to see him. But he would quickly know how upset and worried she had become when he failed to contact her after so many months.

Traffic moved quickly and the drive through Michigan, Indiana and the city allowed Moira to make the trip back to Evanston in record time. She pulled into the driveway and surveyed the property. Things always appear different upon a person's return from vacation, she thought. She pulled the car into the garage, got her luggage out of the trunk and proceeded to the back door. She didn't notice the figure inside the house standing in the kitchen next to the refrigerator. She put her bags down, unlocked the door and went inside. Moira was shocked and then excited when she saw Bartlett's grinning face looking at her. She waited for several seconds, then dropped her bags and slowly walked over to him, tears forming in her eyes. "Where the hell have you been?" she asked, beginning to cry, holding him and slugging his chest. "I have been so worried about you. All this time you've never written ... called or anything. Damn you," she said. Then she put her arms around him, hugged and kissed him as tears poured down her face.

"I know," he said. "I'm sorry. I can explain. I'll make it up to you honey," he said.

He held her for what seemed like an hour until finally she released herself from him, backed away and said, "I've been waiting for over a year and a half. Jimmy, why haven't I heard from you? Where have you been and what have you been doing?"

"Before I tell you anything I need to know one thing," Bartlett said.

"What is that?"

"Will you marry me?"

Moira heard the four important words that she had longed for him to say to her months prior to his disappearance. God, what a time to ask, she thought. *He's a very difficult man and that's why I love him.* "Maybe," she said. Then she began to sob again. "I would have before, but now I'm not sure. I need time to think." *My God, do I want someone who will come and go without a word for months, maybe years at a time?*

After several more minutes of hugging, Bartlett said, "It's good to be back with you. I've made it very difficult for you, haven't I? Under the circumstances, I guess I wouldn't blame you a bit if you never wanted to see me again. Please, let me try to explain ... I've been working with the U.S. government ... that much I can tell you. It has been dangerous work but the work will be ending ... ending very soon. I just need a little more time to conclude my special arrangements and the work will be over. I am financially able to retire, I own a small business and I have moved to a tropical island. It is imperative for mine and your continued safety that my business with the U.S. Government never be discussed with anyone else."

"So, in other words, even if I say 'yes I'll marry you,' then you won't be able to discuss the events of the past year or so with me? Is that correct?"

"Yes. I wish it didn't have to be this way but it can't be avoided. Maybe I shouldn't have contacted you this soon since my return? I got back late Wednesday evening. I came here as quickly as I could. I'll give you all the time you want. Would you like me to leave?"

"Leave! Jimmy, I have been waiting for you to return to me for the past 18 months. I guess I am just slightly confused. I love you, but I need to know you feel the same about me. After all, it has been a long time since we were together. Have your feelings changed?"

"No. I still love you very much. Nothing's changed. Why would I have asked you to marry me if it were otherwise? I brought you a dozen red roses sitting on the table along with your favorite perfume and a box of homemade chocolates."

Moira glanced at the table and the gifts and said, "God, this is such a shock! I expected you to return ... but not so unannounced ... and I never expected a proposal like this. You really know how to turn a person upside down and I mean fast. I want to say 'yes,' but I think we both need more time to rethink our relationship. Don't we?"

"No, I guess I don't. Will you at least consider coming with me on vacation for a week or so?"

"I just got back from vacation. I've got a job ... I've been gone for a week." *God, everything is happening so fast, I don't know what to do or say.*

"I understand. I have made things difficult for you. I want to be with you now and I want to make up for the past. Please come with me. I want you to see my island. You'll love it there. It's almost as beautiful as you," Bartlett said, putting his arm around her waist and slowly leading her toward the bedroom. "You're tired from the drive. We can talk in bed."

Bartlett closed the door and they quickly disrobed and climbed into bed. They lay still for a short while, talked and then gradually began to passionately kiss.

* * *

Monday morning at 6:30, Moira emerged from the bathroom dressed and ready for work. She awoke Bartlett by lightly touching his brow and kissed him first on the cheek and then on the lips. "Good morning honey," she said, sitting on the bed next to him. "The past few days have been wonderful."

"I think so, too. I love you," he said, gently kissing her.

"I've got to go to work now, but we can talk more when I get home tonight."

"Moira, I have to leave for Washington this afternoon to conclude my business. It should take a few days and then I'll be ready to go home. I'd like to take you with me to the island. What do you say?"

"Oh, Jimmy, I want to say yes, but I can't decide this quickly. There's so much to do. I've got the house and my job. I'm not like you. I have to think and be sure it's right for me. I'd have to quit my job, sell the house, move ..."

"You love me don't you?"

"Yes I do ... but I need more time too ..."

"I'll tell you what. I'll be waiting for you at the Miami International Airport this Saturday morning. There is a late afternoon flight to St. Croix from there. I'll get us first class tickets. St. Croix is only a few hours flying time from there. Spend a week with me on the island. The weather is perfect there and we'll have time to talk, sightsee and enjoy ourselves. Anytime you want to leave there are plenty of flights back to Chicago connecting through Miami. What do you say?"

"Well, I'd like to but, I'd have to get approval from my boss. You drive me crazy! You know that don't you?" Moira said as she kissed him again on the lips. "When will I hear from you if you're going to D.C. this afternoon?"

"I'll call you tonight from there ... we can talk for an hour if you want."

"OK honey," she said. "But don't you ever leave me again like you did before. Promise?"

"Yes, I promise."

"Now, give me a hug and a kiss," she said as they embraced for several moments. "Have a safe flight. I've got to go now or else I'll be late for work."

"Bye, honey," Bartlett said. "I'll call you tonight."

"Goodbye," she said, hurriedly walking out of the room.

A moment later he heard the back screen door close and the car pulling out of the garage. The house had been filled with life when she was home, but after she left he felt alone as he had before. He knew he didn't like feeling alone; that was his constant thought.

He remembered when he was in Vietnam and the emptiness he felt being there. There were lots of soldiers in his company, but he had gotten close to only two. Gentry and Killian. Now they were both gone, Moira was gone and he was alone again.

*   *   *

Bartlett took time packing his bag. He had plenty of cash from the job and clean clothes, thanks to Moira. He probably would need some equipment for New Orleans, but it would be easy to buy things there.

He poured himself a glass of milk and then called for a cab. He slowly shut the front door and walked toward the awaiting taxi, and then stared back at the home. He wondered if he would ever be in Chicago or at the house again. He decided before leaving for New Orleans to visit his parents grave to say his final goodbyes.

The cabbie waited for him at the cemetery and then delivered him to O'Hare International Airport. Bartlett was ready to return to New Orleans. There was some unfinished business to handle and a sizable amount of cash needed to be retrieved from several area banks. *I can hardly wait to avenge Benny's untimely death.*

Chapter 40

The late afternoon flight from Chicago to New Orleans took over two hours. Bartlett was feeling more at ease than he had in years when he stepped off the plane. His last assignment was over and he had been reunited with Moira. In two nearby parish banks was a $200,000 stash waiting for him to retrieve. Getting his cash out of a safety deposit box would be quick and easy, but dealing with Aguilar would be another matter.

He regretted having to deceive Moira further, but it was a necessary evil. He didn't want to explain the New Orleans trip to her. The Washington story was at least consistent with his previous tale.

Under other circumstances, Bartlett would not have bothered with Aguilar but there was more than Gentry's death to consider. Aguilar was a constant worry, because he had placed a substantial bounty on Bartlett's life. In addition, his emotional connection to Gentry was substantial. They had been good friends and loyal business partners. Gentry had saved his life once in

Vietnam and he had helped Bartlett become Emery Clements, owner/operator of SC Marketing.

When Bartlett learned Aguilar was directly responsible for the brutal execution of Gentry, he decided there needed to be retribution. It was obvious Gentry had kept his mouth shut concerning Emery Clements. He had paid the highest price anyone could pay for a friendship; he sacrificed his life. Bartlett felt he might have encountered Aguilar long before now if Gentry had told everything he knew about Bartlett.

He owed Gentry a debt of gratitude for his silence, because when he stole Aguilar's cash he had in effect sold out Gentry. In spite of the fact, Gentry was now gone and he wanted the debt to somehow be repaid.

Bartlett knew finding Aguilar wouldn't be too difficult, because Gentry had provided him with personal information about the drug dealer's whereabouts. He had a working knowledge of Gentry's operation and the prior responsibilities he performed for Aguilar. Aguilar was the typical drug dealer; he liked cash, sexy women and had an overabundance of expensive toys.

Aguilar had a reputation for being brutal and most knew he would kill anyone who got in his way. The allure of the drug experience had finally gotten to the man. He had become a frequent user of his own product and now, at times, acted crazily.

Aguilar lived in a beautifully restored and expensively decorated antebellum mansion just outside of New

Orleans. He ran his business affairs from an old riverside warehouse facility about five blocks upstream from the French Quarter. He was a visible and flamboyant dresser who always had at least one attractive blond or redhead at his side. He regularly lunched at several of the finer French restaurants in the Quarter.

Bartlett could always find Aguilar, but he knew Aguilar would be difficult to kill. His entourage included women, associates and several bodyguards. Bartlett had thought about how he might eliminate the whole bunch. The women were excluded from the plan, but the rest could go. Aguilar was a dangerous criminal. His drug business had inflicted pain and suffering on lots of people, including Benjamin Gentry. Killing Aguilar would be considered by most to be a grand public service. If he tried to kill Aguilar, his involvement would once again put him into jeopardy. After the last assignment, he had decided, it would be wise to avoid killing all together. If he didn't take his own advice, Bartlett thought, he might get caught or possibly killed.

His thoughts drifted back to the assassination of Alderman Brezinski and the problems associated with mixing his business and personal concerns. *Maybe I should look for another way to deal with Aguilar and without my direct personal involvement.*

Bartlett learned through the vast New Orleans criminal network that a rogue cop named Toussaint had been assigned to the SC Marketing murder case. He had never met Toussaint, but he recalled Gentry discussing the man and his preference for young, good-looking women. He remembered Gentry saying Toussaint provided drugs to women, mostly exotic dancers, in return for sexual favors.

In the past, he knew Gentry and Aguilar had made regular payments to the New Orleans police department. The payments ensured the local narcotics task force would look the other way concerning their drug activities in the city. Toussaint had been assigned to collect the payoffs from Gentry's distribution operation.

Bartlett figured Toussaint was probably upset with Aguilar for getting rid of Gentry. It was rumored Toussaint's new contact had continued his regular cash payoff but had reduced his personal drug supply. In addition, according to the source, Toussaint's criminal investigation concerning Clements and SC Marketing had been halted within the department. His efforts and the investigation had been stopped due to a lack of interest from the prosecutor's office.

Bartlett assumed Toussaint was still on Aguilar's payroll, but he wondered if all the pertinent details of the investigation had been passed to Aguilar. He was sure Aguilar had paid Toussaint very well for any information about the case.

Bartlett wondered if Aguilar's $100,000 bounty on Emery Clements might have caused Toussaint to be less than forthright with him or maybe he had. Bartlett thought the first possibility was more likely. Toussaint probably wanted to find Clements himself and claim the reward. Bartlett thought it might be interesting to see what would happen to Toussaint, if he fed information about the Clements case directly to Aguilar.

At 11:30 Monday evening, Bartlett rented a cheap motel room not far from the New Orleans airport. He got a bite to eat at an open-all-night greasy spoon and retired for eight hours of needed rest. By mid-morning Tuesday, Bartlett had formulated a strategy to deal with Aguilar. He decided to contact Manuel Bolero, Aguilar's second in command, in order to pass information to Aguilar.

Bartlett had recorded Bolero's private number in a coded book he used when he worked with Gentry. He made the call to Bolero. The buzzer rang repeatedly until Bolero picked up the receiver. "Hello," he said.

"Is this Manuel Bolero?" Bartlett asked.

"Yes. Who is this?"

"A friend."

"What do you want, friend," said Bolero.

"Are you interested in new information about Emery Clements?"

"What do you have?"

"Toussaint has been holding out on you. He has valuable information about Clements. Information that will help guide you to him and your stolen cash."

"Really," said Bolero.

"Yes, he has information about Clements that no one else possesses except me. Ask him about Clements' connection to Chicago and JBS Consulting. Ask him about Frank Russo, the man who ran JBS for Emery Clements. Incidentally, Clements is also known as John Bartkowski, an old Vietnam veteran buddy of the late Benjamin Gentry."

"Do you know anything else?"

"No, but I think Toussaint might."

"What can we do for you?"

"Nothing. I'm a friend. I'll reveal myself to you in time. Fair enough?"

"OK, many thanks friend," Bolero said as he hung up the receiver.

* * *

Ten minutes after receiving the unexpected phone call, Bolero was able to speak with Aguilar. Bolero relayed the caller's message. Aguilar was furious. He instructed Bolero to locate Toussaint and request a private meeting at his warehouse that evening. Bolero was told to avoid any mention of the informant or the phone conversation to Toussaint.

* * *

It had been another miserable weather day in New Orleans. Toussaint hated the moisture, heat and humidity of the region, regardless of being born and raised in Louisiana. The steady rain had come down in buckets for most of the morning and early afternoon. Toussaint had received Bolero's call around 3. He planned to meet with Aguilar at 7 that evening. Earlier, he had made plans to see his favorite young lady friend for dinner and sex. He hoped the meeting didn't go too long because his date was at 8.

Toussaint had no idea what Aguilar wanted from him, but he knew better than to refuse a request from the drug dealer. He was sure Aguilar wanted something and he hoped there would be money in it for him.

At a quarter till 7, Toussaint pulled his unmarked cruiser into the gravel drive of the warehouse. Outside he was greeted by two toughs, who asked to see his identification. They frisked him and immediately took possession of his revolver.

He was escorted to a side door by one of the men, who unlocked the door and led him inside the building. In the shadows, toward the rear of the building, Toussaint could see Aguilar's expensive black Mercedes.

The warehouse was dark, humid and empty with the exception of the vehicle and a stairway leading to an upstairs room. When Toussaint entered the building, he could see Aguilar at the top of the stairs. "Come upstairs," invited Aguilar.

"Sure, Mr. Aguilar."

Inside the office, Toussaint was impressed by the plushness of the interior. Antique chairs, fancy brass light fixtures, beautiful paintings and an enormous mahogany desk adorned the room. "Sit down. We need to talk," Aguilar told him, pointing to an upholstered chair in front of the desk.

Toussaint sat down and stared intently at Aguilar.

"Do you drink?" asked Aguilar.

"Not before dinner, thanks."

"Do you know why Bolero called this meeting?"

"No sir."

"We got a call from an informant today who said you know more than you're telling us about Emery Clements. Is he right?"

Toussaint had already begun to feel uncomfortable in the muggy building, even before Aguilar's questioning began. After Aguilar mentioned Clements' name, Toussaint began to shift nervously in his seat; his forehead, checks and neck were flushed and small beads of sweat formed on his brow. Toussaint remained silent, almost comatose, as several seconds passed. Aguilar stayed calm at first, but he quickly became impatient with Toussaint's silence. Frustrated, Aguilar arose from his seat, walked around the desk and confronted Toussaint who was seated in front of the desk. Aguilar looked at him directly and said again, in a louder tone, "Is he right?"

After another second or two passed, Toussaint answered, "I'm not sure ... I think I've kept you up to date."

"Well then, who the hell is Frank Russo?"

"He's a local small-time Chicago hood who ran JBS Consulting, a personnel consulting business," spurted Toussaint.

"Who owns JBS?"

"I'm not sure."

"Is the business connected to Clements?"

"I don't know ... I plan to interview Russo myself later."

"Our informant says Clements is behind JBS Consulting. What do you think?"

"I don't know."

"Why didn't you tell me about Russo before now?"

"I guess I thought I had."

With that remark, Aguilar became enraged. He grabbed Toussaint and produced a long stiletto knife. He put the open blade into the side of Toussaint's neck and said, "Don't ever lie to me. You never told me about Russo, you sonofabitch. Don't you ever lie to me again."

Toussaint had tried to jump out of the chair until he felt the sharp edge of the blade pierce the skin on his neck. He was startled to see several drops of his blood, drip down upon his shirt sleeve. He could feel the presence of

Aguilar's bodyguard holding him down from behind.

"I'm sorry ... ," Toussaint said, stricken with fear.

"It's OK," said Aguilar, now in a more relaxed tone, as he gradually released his grip on the man. "You're a lucky cop, Toussaint. I've paid you and the department well over the years. But I have kept very good records, just in case I want to prove it," Aguilar said. He paused momentarily, looked deeply into Toussaint's eyes, and said, "Understand?"

At that point, Toussaint had become so emotionally upset and frightened that he could only move his head up and down to confirm his understanding.

"Listen to me ... if you ever hold out on me again you'll pay heavily," said Aguilar.

"I'm sorry," said Toussaint once again nervously moving his head. "I won't."

"Yes, I know you won't," said Aguilar, as he slowly patted the detective on the shoulder. "Now, where can I find Russo?"

"He's in Chicago. I have his address in my files. I can get it for you."

"I want it tonight."

"I'll get it," Toussaint said, still shaken from the experience.

"Now, get out of here ... call Bolero with the address later."

"Yes, sir," said Toussaint. He felt lucky he had averted a huge problem with Aguilar for holding out on him. He had been given a serious threat and a warning. As he hurriedly departed the room, he wondered about the informant. Toussaint hardly looked back as he swiftly raced down the stairs, passed through the exit door and headed for the false security of his parked cruiser. He couldn't get the cruiser started quickly enough to leave the area. He squealed the tires as he pulled out onto the street. He hadn't been that scared in a long time.

Later he was angry and anxious. His thoughts returned to Aguilar. That scumbag almost killed me, he thought, and over some two-bit criminal in Chicago. I should fix him good for putting a knife to my throat, scaring the shit out of me and threatening the department. *He could have easily cut my throat.* That sonofabitch should know better than to mess with the cops.

Toussaint was sure Aguilar would do anything, including killing a cop, to find Clements. Aguilar had made a veiled threat to him and the department, concerning the payoff records.

If Aguilar ever passed his records to the Feds, a lot of his fellow officers and some judges would lose their jobs and their families and go to jail. He would relay Aguilar's threat to his boss. *If Aguilar thinks he's invincible, he's wrong. Maybe it's time to take Aguilar down before he can do any collateral damage. Maybe Aguilar has developed a false sense of security. Maybe it's time to get rid of that sonofabitch and put Bolero in his place.*

Toussaint knew drug lords like Aguilar existed because of the enormous public demand. The problem was amplified by crooked cops and judges who protected the dealers. Without them and the protection they afforded, Aguilar's operation would have crumbled. Aguilar would be caught and sent to jail. *Maybe Aguilar needed to be reminded of the consequences of threatening the police.*

When Toussaint got back to his office, he grabbed a small flask of bourbon stashed in his drawer and took a couple of big swigs. The booze seemed to relax him. He called Bolero with Russo's address. Bolero seemed pleased to have the information and acted as if everything was fine. Everything wasn't fine. He would talk to his boss in the morning about Aguilar's threat.

* * *

At quarter till 8, Toussaint walked into the station house, got a second cup of coffee and knocked on his captain's office door. "Good morning, captain. I need to see you for 10 minutes or so, if it's convenient," Toussaint said.

"Sure, come on in, sit down Toussaint. What do you need?"

"I got a call from Bolero, one of Aguilar's top men, yesterday afternoon. He said Aguilar wanted to meet with me last evening. I figured he wanted some information. I didn't know what kind, but I was partially right. He wanted to know about a lead I had uncovered in Chicago concerning the SC Marketing murder case."

"Did you cooperate?"

"I did, but apparently not well enough. He got mad, real mad. He pulled a knife on me and stuck me with it. It just pierced the skin. I thought he was going to slit my throat. I was really scared."

"Yes, go on."

"Then, out of the blue, he said he had kept good records concerning the drug payoffs to us. Said he could prove them to the Feds, if he wanted."

"What was that all about?"

"I don't know. Maybe, he was just trying to push his weight around. I gave him what he wanted. Look, you should have seen him. He acted crazily. He had a deranged look in his eyes. He uses his own stuff, you know."

"I didn't know."

"Maybe he's gotten too independent and out of control. After this threat, I wonder if we can trust him anymore. Maybe we should work with Bolero. Last month he told our informant he was ready to take over."

"Who's the informant?"

"Pablo, our undercover guy. Bolero told him he thinks Aguilar is slipping. Lately, he says, he's been concentrating more on his own drug use, women and toys rather than business. He's gotten sloppy."

"What do we know about this Bolero?"

"Pablo told me he's OK, for a bad guy."

"Well, I don't have a problem with it, as long as this Bolero remembers who helped get him there. Will he increase our take?"

"Yeah. I think so."

"OK, then. You take care of it. Put a team together with our people; cops we know we can trust."

"Sounds good."

"Keep it simple, Toussaint, not too messy. It needs to look like a hit."

"I understand."

*   *   *

Two days later, according to a lead story in the Times-Picayune, Hector Aguilar, reputed to be the New Orleans drug kingpin, was reportedly found dead at his rural home. According to the account, a maid discovered the body, face down, floating in the swimming pool. Aguilar had been shot once in the head by an unknown assailant while taking a late night swim. The police believed the murder weapon was a .22-caliber pistol. Local speculation is Aguilar was killed as a result of an internal power struggle, within the drug community. A top Aguilar man,

Manuel Bolero, who had been out of town at the time of the killing, appears to have emerged as his replacement.

*   *   *

Bartlett arose Thursday morning and was surprised to read about Aguilar's demise on the front page of the newspaper. He wondered if Toussaint had been involved in the assassination. Apparently, his idea to stir up trouble between Aguilar and Toussaint had worked and much better than he had envisioned. Aguilar must have put an immense amount of pressure on Toussaint in order to wind up dead. He couldn't believe his luck.

Bartlett's business was abruptly concluded in New Orleans and ahead of schedule. He packed his bag, checked out of the motel and called for a cab.

On his way to the airport, Bartlett stopped at a postal substation, located in a strip mall. He instructed the cabbie to wait as he mailed a small, rectangular-shaped box.

Chapter 41

Several weeks after his reappearance, Bartlett and Moira were eating Sunday brunch on the veranda of The Salty Pirate, a seaside resort near Christiansted.

Scanning the horizon, Moira admired the clear blue water and the gorgeous landscape view from the veranda. She was intoxicated with St. Croix and she loved sharing her time there with him.

She was lost in a daydream when the waitress appeared with a second round of Bloody Mary's. "Did you enjoy our brunch?" the waitress asked.

"It was wonderful," Moira responded quickly, with a smile. "I especially liked the grouper."

"You can have fresh grouper here every day of your life," Bartlett stated, "if you want."

"I'm not sure I could prepare it as well as they do," she said. "It was very delicious."

"You'd learn."

"Ma'am, can I get you anything else?" asked the waitress.

"Do you have newspapers here?" asked Moira.

"Yes, national or local?"

"National. I like to keep informed you know," she said, smiling brightly at Bartlett. "Even on vacation."

Several minutes later, the waitress returned with a coffee pot and a folded Miami Herald under her arm.

"Anybody want coffee?"

"We'll both have coffee and she'll take the paper," Bartlett said.

The waitress poured a large cup of coffee for each of them and handed the newspaper to Moira.

"Thanks," Moira said as the waitress began clearing the table.

Moira picked up the Herald and began scanning the front page. Bartlett finished his coffee, excused himself and headed for the restroom. When he returned, he wasn't surprised to find Moira still engrossed in the newspaper.

After a second cup and several more minutes, Bartlett was becoming slightly bored and impatient. "Ready to go, honey?" he asked nicely.

"Sure, I'm ready if you are," she said, folding the newspaper and following him toward the stairs. As they passed the hostess station, Moira handed the newspaper to the woman and said, "Thanks."

"You're welcome ma'am. Have a nice day," the hostess responded, as they descended the steps and walked to the Jeep.

Several minutes later, they arrived in downtown Christiansted and decided to shop for casual clothing. The couple located a small boutique and a half hour later emerged with several packages stuffed full of clothing. Moira placed the packages in the back seat of the Jeep.

On the way home, Bartlett decided to stop at the local grocery to get some food to eat for breakfast. Once inside, Moira located a news rack with the same issue of the Herald she had been reading. She placed the paper in the cart along with eggs, milk, cheese and sausage.

"Didn't you read the newspaper cover to cover at brunch, honey?" asked Bartlett, slightly smiling when he noticed the Miami Herald in the cart.

"Not quite," she said. "There's several stories I want to finish reading. One in particular I'll tell you about on the drive back home."

In the Jeep, Moira grabbed the paper from the shopping bag and said, "I'll need to finish reading the story first before I can tell you about it. It's amazing actually."

"What's the story about?" asked Bartlett, turning on to the highway.

"The mob," she proclaimed. "You won't believe what happened."

"Oh, you might be surprised," he said, looking over and smiling at her.

Several minutes later, she announced, "OK, I'm done."

"So, what's it about."

"Well, it's about a mob boss from Detroit. His name is Dominic Ricci. He has been implicated in a plot to kill a Michigan legislator and his girlfriend. The remarkable part is the hit man who was hired to do the job provided a tape recording with incriminating information including conversations between he and the gangster's attorney. The authorities think he may have altered the sound of his voice on the tape. According to the article, the attorney hired the hit man to do the job, at the request of Ricci. The authorities received a cassette tape in the mail and interviewed the attorney, who quickly gave up Ricci in return for immunity from prosecution."

"Is the attorney named?"

"Wallace … Henry Wallace. Apparently, he is a well-known, respected attorney in Detroit," she exclaimed.

"Not anymore," said Bartlett. "What do they say happened to the hit man?"

"They haven't located him yet. Wallace stated he had contacted the hit man through JBS Consulting, a Chicago-based firm. The business is now defunct. They are looking for a man named Russo, who supposedly ran the business. He's been missing for at least a week."

They will never find Russo. He is missing alright and

for good.

"According to the story, the hit man kidnapped them from their bedroom, at the senator's Lake Michigan home in Saugatuck. He drove them to an old, rental farmhouse in an isolated area. He put both of them in separate, shallow graves and fired blanks at them as they lay bound in the holes. Of course, they were scared to death. According to the senator, the hit man said he faked their killings so they would understand what would have happened with another killer. He staged the mock killing in the hopes that they would seriously heed his warning. He apologized but said he was just trying to save their lives. The hit man advised them to stay in hiding for at least a week, until it would be safe for them to contact the authorities. They were provided with food, water, sleeping bags and a cell phone by the hit man.

"The hit man explained he was being set up for a double-cross by the mob boss; so instead he double-crossed them. God, what a plot."

"Yeah, it's really hard to imagine how it could have happened. Sounds to me like the hit man was quite skilled and ingenious, don't you think?"

"It sure does," said Moira.

"I'll bet he was being well paid to do the job, but the mob boss made a big mistake; he should have never tried to double-cross the hit man. Looks like they are going to pay dearly for the mistake."

"I wonder if they'll ever catch the hit man?"

"I doubt it. Sounds like he was very intelligent and resourceful," Bartlett said, pulling into the driveway. "Doesn't sound like he is really that bad of a guy after all, does it?"

"Well, I don't know," she said. "Can a hit man change?"

"Anybody can change if they want to," Bartlett said.

"I guess you are right, Jimmy."

"How about we go to the beach for a quick swim before we take an afternoon nap? I want to be rested before we go out for the evening."

"Well … as long as we sleep," she said, smiling brightly at Bartlett. "Sure. You know it's really hot today and a swim sounds great," she added, leaning over and lightly kissing him on the cheek. "I'm so happy we can finally be together," Moira said, gently squeezing his hand.

"Me too," Bartlett said. "It wasn't easy, but I think being with you is just what I have been missing." *My battles and wars are finally over.*